"I should have known a redhead would demand action," Jules said

"You have lovely hair," Jules insisted.

"Thank you." She heard the stiffness in her words. But he'd been the one to put the desk between them, reminding her that she was his employee.

Still, it warmed her that he liked her hair.

"Martha...."

She looked up and met Jules's eyes, and her breath caught.

The door flew open. "Aha—there you are!" Cathleen whirled into the room and perched on the desk. "Jules, I absolutely must have help this evening."

"Come on, I'll go with you," Martha said quickly.

Once they had left the library, Cathleen grasped Martha's arm. "If you know what's good for you, you'll leave Jules alone."

"I'm not—"

"Don't come over all smarmy with me the way you do with him. I'm no fool. I can tell what you're up to. Keep away from him if you want to stay at Black Tor."

RESTLESS OBSESSION

JANE TOOMBS

Harlequin Books

TORONTO • NEW YORK • LONDON
AMSTERDAM • PARIS • SYDNEY • HAMBURG
STOCKHOLM • ATHENS • TOKYO • MILAN

Published July 1984
ISBN 0-373-32005-1

CHAPTER ONE

THE BREEZE BLEW STREAMERS OF MIST across the gray water to hang a tattered curtain of dampness between the ferry and Seattle. Martha Jamison turned and walked to the foredeck, where she stood almost alone, peering into the grayness surrounding the boat.

"It'll clear before you reach the island," the Seattle taxi driver had insisted. "They get the best of our weather over there." As though weather were a commodity the Canadians were guilty of hoarding.

Martha touched her hair nervously. Ginetha had helped her do it up in a French knot that morning, but the mist was encouraging stray wisps to curl out of the neat arrangement. The hairdo had been an attempt to seem as "mature" as possible, to fit the ad description. Perhaps she should go back inside?

"Ever been to Victoria?"

Martha turned to face a bearded young man.

"No."

"You'll like Vancouver Island, but don't stay just in Victoria. The city's a marvel, but if you really want to...."

Martha recognized the glint in his blue eyes and decided to be blunt. "My plans are all made," she said. "Someone's meeting me." Her tone was crisp. She was not one to encourage stray admirers. She turned her back to the young man.

A shaft of sunlight had cut through the overcast and

glinted on the water. A sea gull rode a small chunk of drift-wood.

"There's two of us facing the future, at least," the bearded man remarked.

So he hadn't left. Martha said nothing.

"I like to think of the ferry as a world microcosm. Hardly original, I'm afraid," the man went on. "By the way, I'm Branwell Lowrey—my friends call me Bran."

She didn't respond.

"Well, anyway, we brave spirits here at the bow are looking ahead. The people aft are those still caught in the past, while the few along the sides live for today."

Am I facing the future? Martha asked herself. *Isn't this trip a flight from reality, as Ginetha says?* She shook her head.

"You don't agree?" Bran asked.

She turned to him, ashamed of her rudeness.

"I don't know," she said. He was a good-looking man with chiseled features and would probably be equally attractive without the beard, unlike some men she'd met. His eyes smiled when he did.

I can at least talk to him, she told herself. Ginetha's admonitions rang in her ears. *"You can't wrap yourself in memories of Johann forever. His death didn't make him a saint. Let other men have a chance in your life."* Martha gazed dispassionately at Branwell Lowrey.

"Where did you get all those freckles?" he asked.

"From my father." Her reply was automatic for she'd been answering that question since childhood.

"Your freckles aren't all over, are they?" Johann had asked on their wedding night. They weren't, of course. Martha clenched her teeth and tried to listen to Bran.

"I'm Irish," he said. "Only second-generation American, would you believe?"

"Scottish," she said. "A long time ago."

"What's your name?"

"Martha Jamison." After Johann had died, she'd taken her maiden name again to thrust everything away. But Johann still lived in her mind—Johann and their days together.

"You're certainly not one of the dark dour Scots."

"No, I'm the sandy kind."

"Will you be staying long?" Bran asked.

"I—I'm not sure." Ginetha thought she was crazy for answering the ad in the first place, and maybe Ginetha was right.

Martha studied Bran, bearded and tanned, in his jeans and T-shirt. What would it be like to throw a few necessities in a backpack and wander wherever one chose? She'd seen the group of young people come aboard with their packs. Bran looked as if he belonged with them. She was no older than Bran, surely. Twenty-eight shouldn't be too old to—to what? To be happy?

Martha straightened her shoulders and stared out over the bow. From the way the sun had broken through the weather was obviously clearing, and the sullen water was changing to a brownish blue as more of the sky appeared. Land became visible—pine-covered hills.

"That's Vancouver Island," Bran said. "We're almost there."

A sailboat passed to their left, its white sails taut in the crisp breeze. Other small boats skirted the shoreline.

"Salmon fishing," Bran explained. "This is the season."

Gray-and-brown gulls swooped low over the ferry, seeming to eye her curiously. The island grew larger, and she could identify houses, a church spire. No, perhaps not a church at all, the rambling white building with the tower up the middle, its peaked roof resembling a spire. That wasn't a cross at the tip but a—was it a porpoise? A whale?

Then the boat entered the harbor inlet, and she had a confused impression of piers, warehouses, the loud roar of a seaplane taking off, a train whistle, the hoot of the ferry, foreign flags flying. But of course in this place *she* was the foreigner—the flags were Canadian.

"You'll never get the job," Ginetha had insisted, the *Seattle Post-Intelligencer* spread on the rug between them, open to the help-wanted ads. Ginetha had been eager for Martha to stay, to find a job in Seattle and not return to what she termed "the nightmare of L.A."

L.A. was all right, Martha thought. It kept her hidden. But Ginetha hadn't let her alone, bombarding her with phone calls and letters and threatening to come in person if Martha didn't stop moping around in "that depressing apartment—how you can stay there after what happened...?"

But the apartment was the known, and Martha had been afraid to leave it, until Ginetha had suddenly appeared and carted her off to Seattle.

"Listen to this." Ginetha read ads for office nurses, ICU nurses, private-duty nurses. "Take your pick."

"I don't think I'm ready, Gin." Panic rose in Martha at the thought of monitoring the ICU machines, making quick decisions, reassuring frightened patients and relatives.

"Oh, don't be silly. Once a nurse, always a nurse. When we worked together at Camarillo you were better than anyone else on the floor, and you know it."

Martha had met Ginetha at Camarillo State Hospital when they'd been fresh out of training. Ginetha was from Oregon, Martha from Arizona. They'd taken their state civil-service exam for psychiatric nursing together. Then Martha had met Johann and married him.

"I haven't worked for four years," Martha reminded Ginetha.

Ginetha waved her protest away and continued to scan the paper. "Here's an impossible one. Listen. 'Mature nurse with psychiatric experience to act as companion for young woman. Must live in.'"

"Why 'impossible'?" Martha had asked.

"Because it's on the island and that's Canada and you can't work over there without years of red tape. Anyway, who'd want to live in with a crazy?"

"Let me see the ad."

"Oh, Martha, you don't want anything like that. Either they have a retarded kid that's gotten too big to handle, or else a schiz. I'd think—" Ginetha broke off.

Martha said nothing at all, knowing that they both were thinking of Johann. But there was no use dwelling on the past. "I'm going to answer this ad," Martha told Ginetha.

The reply to her letter had been prompt but imperious: "Please bring your luggage so there will be no delay should the interview prove to be mutually satisfactory." "Jules Garrard," the signature read, and a ferry ticket for the *Princess Margarita* was enclosed.

Even at the moment, with the boat gliding into the dock at Victoria, Martha wasn't sure why she'd persisted in applying for the position. Wasn't Ginetha right? Living-in with any patient could be tiresome, and someone mentally ill might well prove to be impossible. Especially after Johann.

Why did she think she'd be able to handle it? Or want to? Did she crave the security of having a house to live in, of having other people be responsible for supplying her basic needs? No jockeying for position on a hospital staff, no infighting, no battling traffic to work and back. Still, she could have done private duty in Seattle....

"That's the Empress Hotel you're staring at," Bran said.

"What?" She'd been so lost in her interior monologue

that she hadn't realized what she was seeing. "Oh, you mean the building with all the towers and turrets?"

"Yes. And to the right are the legislative buildings."

"The middle one looks like a state capitol."

"Victoria *is* the capital of British Columbia."

"Oh, that's right. Well...." Martha turned from the rail and started toward the cabin. She must smooth her hair before she got off the ferry. First impressions were important. "Goodbye," she called over her shoulder to Bran, then moved a little faster, hoping he wouldn't follow.

In the women's lounge she checked her appearance in the mirror, quickly tucking loose ends of hair into place. She wore no makeup except for pale coral lipgloss. She'd been sleeping well this past week that she'd spent with Ginetha in Seattle—her eyes were clear, their color enhanced by the delft blue of her jacket.

She joined the line of disembarking passengers, her stomach knotted with nervousness. Why was she there at all? The rest of the people around her seemed to be tourists. There were some of the backpackers now, though Bran wasn't in sight. When the customs inspector asked for identification, she showed her driver's license and said she wasn't sure how long she'd be staying in Victoria—perhaps just overnight.

Then she was out of the ferry shed, suitcases in hand. WELCOME TO VICTORIA was spelled out in flowers, marigolds, on the bank to her right. She took a deep breath.

"Miss Jamison?"

Martha turned and saw a middle-aged man with graying hair in a fringe around an otherwise bald head. He held a cap in his hand that matched his gray uniform.

"Yes."

He put on his hat and plucked the bags from her hands. With a nod he indicated a gray Rolls-Royce. "This is the car, miss. My name is Henry."

A chauffeur, yet, she thought after being shut into the back seat. But what else should she expect of a family wealthy enough to hire a live-in psychiatric nurse? The wages mentioned in the letter were very generous. "Too generous," Ginetha had said. "This patient must be a real nut. Why don't you reconsider and stay with me?"

Why hadn't she? Ginetha was an easy girl to be around. She didn't ask questions, although Martha felt them there, dozens of questions coiled in Ginetha's mind like poisonous snakes: "Did he really try to kill you like the papers said? Wasn't it awful when you unlocked the door and found him?"

Martha closed her eyes for a moment. Maybe that's why she hadn't stayed with Ginetha—the unasked questions. Maybe she was avoiding reality by this flight to another country. She'd let her hair grow and wore it differently; she no longer lightened it to blond, as Johann had preferred—she wasn't Marty Collier anymore, Mrs. Johann Collier. She was Martha Jamison, R.N. Who in Canada would connect the two?

They drove along a main street that had lamp posts with five round globes in a cluster like grapes. And baskets of live flowers hung from projections under the globes—geraniums, petunias and lobelia in a riot of reds and pinks and blues. The lamp posts themselves were the same delft blue as her pantsuit.

"Admiring the flowers, miss?"

"Oh, yes. They're lovely."

"We call Victoria the Garden City. September is almost the end of the hanging baskets, though. You ought to see them in the spring."

"Have you lived here long?"

"Ten years now, miss."

Ten years ago I was still in Flagstaff, Martha thought.

Still at home, just getting ready to go away for nurse's training.

"Did you see the house from the ferry?" Henry asked.

"The house?"

"Black Tor, the Garrard place. On your left before you enter the harbor."

"I don't know. I might have."

"There's a rocky point, like. Used to be able to see a black cliff in the early days, I've been told. That's where the house got its name. But the trees and bushes have grown over the black rock."

"I saw one place I thought was a church at first," Martha said. "It had a tower with a figure of a porpoise on a rod at the roof tip."

"Then you did see the house, miss. Only that's a killer whale. Mr. Abel Garrard, who built Black Tor in 1880, had the whale put up there as his little joke. He was an eccentric man by all accounts." As he spoke, Henry turned left off the main road. "The Garrards don't live in Victoria proper, or in Equimalt, either—that's this suburb we've passed through. Black Tor isn't near anything. Isolated, that's what it is."

Martha felt his eyes on her in the rearview mirror.

"I like the country," she said.

"Good for you, miss. Some people don't."

Had Henry driven other applicants to Black Tor? Out and back again when the interviews weren't "mutually satisfactory"?

The car passed between stone pillars, and she caught a glimpse of open iron gates, half hidden by shrubbery.

"We're inside the grounds now," Henry told her. "The family owns forty acres. Like a park it is, mostly."

The drive meandered among old trees that overhung the road, past shrubs and flower beds and came at last to the white house Martha had seen from the boat. Close up, it was a confusing arrangement of wings, ells and additions that had been added in what seemed a completely haphazard fashion. The building was huge, and the effect was not so much amusing as almost frightening, as though a mad architect had executed an insane masterpiece.

Out of the car, Martha craned her neck to stare at the octagonal tower that rose from the center at least four stories high, its steep roof crowned with what Henry had said was a killer whale. An odd choice.

As she gazed upward there came a loud crash, as of glass breaking, and Henry caught her arm, pulling her off balance as an object struck the ground beside her. Martha stifled a scream as she looked down at a cat's mangled body by her feet, slivers of glass stuck in its matted fur. Then she glanced back at the tower in horror.

"Don't be so upset, miss," Henry said. "That's just Miss Josephine's way."

CHAPTER TWO

MARTHA PULLED AWAY from Henry and watched him stoop to gather up the cat. She saw now that there was no blood; in fact, there was a sawdustlike material on the ground where the cat's body had lain.

"It's only a stuffed animal, miss," Henry said. "Miss Josephine sometimes tears them up."

"'Them'?"

"Black Tor has many stuffed animals. All the pets the family ever owned have been preserved this way. And then Mr. Abel was quite a sportsman, so...."

"But she threw the cat from the tower at me!" Martha exclaimed.

"Well, now, not *at* you exactly, miss. Near you, yes. Miss Josephine doesn't want a nurse here, I'm afraid."

Martha stared at Henry. At, near—what was the difference? She felt like getting back in the car and demanding to be driven into Victoria immediately. Why bother with—

"You must be Miss Jamison. Won't you come in?"

Martha whirled to see who'd spoken.

"We've just arrived, sir," Henry said.

The man nodded. His black hair had a white streak on the left side. He was tall, darkly handsome, and he gave her a quick smile that failed to light his eyes. "I'm Jules Garrard," he said to Martha.

"How do you do?" she answered, feeling half hypnotized by his dramatic appearance as she allowed him to show her through the open front door.

"I believe your letter mentioned you'd not been to Canada before," Jules said.

"This is my first visit."

They entered a paneled entry hall. Then the brightness of the day was shut away when Henry came in behind them and closed the door. The dark wood and the stained-glass windows suddenly changed day into a tinted twilight. Martha found her breathing quickening, as though the dimness deprived her of air.

Henry stepped ahead to open an inner door leading to a foyer with a massive copper chandelier hanging from a cathedral ceiling. Martha looked to her left and gasped, astonished at the huge black-and-white animal displayed on a pedestal. What was it? Martha remembered billboards featuring L.A.'s Marineland killer whale and realized what she saw there was a stuffed one, arranged as though leaping from the water. It looked inappropriately happy, seeming to grin at her as she passed. Other sea trophies were mounted along the oak-paneled walls—sailfish and salmon—but the killer whale dwarfed them to insignificance.

Henry disappeared down a hall to the left, going through yet another door. Jules Garrard indicated a passage to her right and then ushered her into a half-paneled room, its upper walls papered with a gold-and-green hunting scene. More trophies crowded the walls, except for one, where books filled the shelves from floor to ceiling.

"Grandfather Abel was more of a sportsman than a reader," Jules said. "This was his library. I find that too much exposure to the room gives me claustrophobia." He spread his hands and smiled.

Martha smiled, too, sharing the feeling and already liking Jules Garrard, with his black-and-white hair and his oddly sad eyes.

"Did your grandfather harpoon the killer whale I saw?"

"No. Actually, the family legend is that he tried to save the whale, which had been wounded somehow. But it died, and so he had it hauled to the taxidermist. Grandpa saw himself and the orca as blood brothers."

"Orca?"

"Scientific name. I've done some research on killer whales—a family interest, you might say."

Martha thought of the mounted animal in the foyer. Black and white, a striking contrast, like Jules's hair. Jules was young—not over forty, certainly. She remembered white streaks in the hair as being hereditary. Had Abel Garrard had the trait, as well? Is that why the orca had fascinated him?

Jules offered her a lyreback chair near a rosewood desk. He then sat behind the desk, and she was reminded that this was an interview. For a few moments Jules had made her forget that he was her prospective employer.

"May I call you Martha?" he asked.

"Please."

"You certainly seem to have every qualification to be Josephine's companion," he said.

"I haven't worked in four years," she said. "I—"

He waved his hand. "I'm pleased to have someone closer to her age applying. Aunt Natalie composed the advertisement, hoping, no doubt, for another of the elderly retirees we've had lately. I've tried to tell Natalie she's wrong—" Jules broke off and shrugged.

"The ad did say 'mature,'" Martha began. "But as I *am* twenty-eight, I thought—"

"I have no doubt you're sufficiently mature," Jules told her, smiling. For the first time his eyes seemed to lighten.

Does he find me attractive? Martha wondered. She was very aware of his gaze. She was also aware of him as a man. Surprised and disconcerted at her response to him, she looked down at her hands.

"It's only fair that you meet Josephine before you decide to stay with us," Jules said.

The repetition of Josephine's name brought back the crash of breaking glass and the stuffed cat landing at her feet. Martha straightened and met Jules's eyes. "Why do you need a psychiatric nurse as her companion?" she asked bluntly.

"Josephine is...unusual," Jules said slowly. "I prefer to have you meet her before I say more." He glanced at his watch. "Have you had lunch?"

"I ate on the boat."

He nodded and got up. As Martha started to rise to her feet, he motioned for her to stay seated. Then he went to the door and opened it.

A tall slender girl stood there, her curly dark hair falling past her shoulders. She had no streak of white. As she came into the room, Martha saw that her eyes were sherry yellow. She wore jeans and a gray sweat shirt. Except that she was prettier, she looked much like the backpackers Martha had seen on the ferry.

"This is Josephine," Jules said. "She's fond of listening outside closed doors."

The girl made a face at him. Then her eyes flicked back to Martha.

"This is Martha Jamison, Josephine," Jules said. "As you can see, you were quite wrong in throwing the cat from the tower to frighten her."

"I thought you'd be old," Josephine told Martha. "You're little, so I thought you were one of the tiny wizened kind, and they're even worse than the fat jolly ones."

"How old are you, Josephine?" Martha asked, deciding to ignore the tower episode.

"I'll be twenty-three next month," Josephine replied. "Then I get half—don't I, Jules?"

"Not until your father dies," a man's voice interjected. As he spoke, he came into the room and bowed slightly toward Martha. "Good afternoon, Miss Jamison," he said, then turned to Josephine. "If you'd wear your glasses, you'd know a pretty woman from an old lady, Josie my girl."

"I don't need glasses," Josephine said. "And don't call me 'Josie.' I was at the top of the tower, looking down. How could I tell? Besides, nobody young ever came before." She smiled at Martha, and her smile was engaging. "If I have to have someone stay with me, I'd just as soon it was you."

"This intruder is our cousin, Charn Wexler," Jules said.

Both Josephine and Jules had disregarded Charn's entering words. Had he meant them as a joke? If so, it was a joke in very bad taste.

"Hello," Martha said. If Charn was "our" cousin, were Jules and Josephine brother and sister? She glanced from one to the other.

"Josephine is my half sister," Jules said, as if reading her mind.

"Daddy wore out two wives," Josephine explained.

Martha blinked, trying to assimilate all the information. Her quick assessment of Josephine revealed no evidence of mental illness. Still, such evidence was often concealed, only to emerge when least expected.

"Why don't you two get out so Martha and I can discuss her staying here," Jules suggested.

"I'll bet you were scared, weren't you?" Josephine said to Martha. "You didn't scream or faint or anything, but—"

"I was startled," Martha admitted. "And horrified, since I thought the cat was alive."

"Oh, I wouldn't hurt a real cat," Josephine said, instantly sounding shocked.

"Come on, Josephine," Charn Wexler began, shepherding her toward the door. "You'll frighten Martha off yet."

"We've a rather informal household," Jules commented when the door was shut once more. "Except for Aunt Natalie, of course. She disapproves of us all, including father."

"Your cousin doesn't resemble you or Josephine," Martha noted.

"Charn belongs to the Wexler branch—heavy on Teutonic fairness, with no suggestion of Indian blood such as the Garrards carry. You'd never think Charn was one-sixteenth Indian. As for you, Martha, based on your name and your strawberry-blond hair—"

He broke off, and she thought for a moment he was going to finger a curl that had drifted out of her chignon. Martha quivered as though he had actually touched her.

"I'd say you were a Scot," Jules finished.

She nodded. His irises were so dark a brown they appeared black. She could hardly see the pupils. She wondered irrelevantly if the orca had black eyes.

"Victoria will like that," Jules went on. "Most of the original settlers here were Scots. Many took Indian wives, as did my ancestor, who happened to be French. I'll show you the old graveyard sometime. The names are interesting."

Martha closed her eyes momentarily and turned away from Jules. She'd tried to have Johann cremated, but that had precipitated even more publicity, and at last she'd given up his body to the others, as she should have given up Johann earlier. The funeral had been a public horror.

"You do intend to stay?" Jules asked. "Obviously Josephine accepts you. She liked none of the others."

" 'Others'?"

Jules sighed. "I'm afraid there's been a parade of companions and would-be companions in and out of the house for the past few years. Aunt Natalie would insist on older women, and Josephine—well, you heard her."

"You've never had a younger woman apply?"

Jules hesitated. "You see, Natalie did the interviewing until her illness. She... eliminated anyone under fifty."

"You haven't told me why Josephine needs a companion."

"She's made three suicide attempts in the past year. Then there's the occult fixation, of course. But she's not a psychotic. Her behavior is sometimes—bizarre, though usually rational in terms of her beliefs."

Martha didn't say anything. Any psychotic behavior could be called normal if judged on the basis of the insane individual's beliefs.

"Josephine leads a rather restricted life at present. She needs someone who understands her, someone versed in psychiatry. And, I've felt, someone near her in age. I do hope you'll stay with her."

What was there to return to if she didn't stay? Martha asked herself. Whatever abnormalities Josephine might later display, on the surface she seemed only a somewhat immature young woman. Why not remain here at Black Tor and try to help her? "What about Josephine's medical care?" she inquired. "You do have a doctor seeing her?"

"A psychiatrist, Dr. Louis Marston. Naturally you'll be talking to him later on."

Martha nodded. "I'd like to stay," she said.

Jules touched her arm lightly. "I know you'll be good for Josephine."

Again Martha was terribly aware of his nearness. "Do—are you—who else lives here?" she asked, hating herself for the awkwardness of the question. If he had a wife, what would she do—turn off her reaction? Turn off a reaction she had no control over? She remembered her total response to Johann, and the memory frightened her. Is that the only way she could react to a man—all or nothing? She eyed Jules warily.

"Matthew—he's Natalie's husband. She's my father's sister, now Natalie Drew. My father's an invalid. He'd enjoy having you around if he felt better—he always had an eye for a pretty girl. Charn, of course, and another cousin, an elderly one from my mother's family—Louella Gallion. And Charn's sister, Cathleen. She's over in the States at present, but she'll be returning. An artist of sorts, our Cathleen. Very mod."

No wife.

"Do you have a family nearby?" Jules asked.

"No. And that reminds me—I do have a friend in Seattle. You wrote me at her address. She seemed to think I'd have a problem working in Canada. Is there anything special I should do?"

"There's nothing you need do. As a private citizen I can hire anyone I choose. I don't know how it would be if you wanted to work as a nurse at a hospital here—perhaps your friend is right. But in this case...." He shrugged. "I'll see to any problems relating to your continued stay in Canada."

All at once she felt far from home. *Home?* she asked herself. *You have no home. Why not Canada?*

"Your parents aren't living?" Jules wanted to know.

Martha shook her head. She'd been a late-in-life only child, her father had passed away when she was in high school and her mother, thank God, had died before the horror of Johann's death.

"You will, of course, be dining with us," Jules said.

She stared at him in surprise before she realized there'd

be servants in a house this size and she wasn't to eat with them. Not only Henry, but a cook, maids and likely a housekeeper, since Jules wasn't married. Unless Natalie acted as such. Martha felt alien. She'd had plenty of money, she and Johann, but they'd lived simply in a condominium apartment with a cleaning woman two days a week. This rambling house had stood there since 1880 and must require a small army of servants to keep up.

"I'll ask Ruth to show you to your room." Jules touched a small panel on the wall and after a moment spoke into it. "She'll meet you in the foyer," he finished.

Ruth was a middle-aged woman who wore a gray uniform with a white apron. Martha, astonished, followed her up the curving staircase. She'd had no idea maids still wore uniforms.

"The aquamarine room will be yours, miss," Ruth told her, indicating an open door off the second-floor hallway.

Martha was relieved to find that the only stuffed animal in the bedroom was a yellow canary in a gilt cage. The room was furnished with heavy oak pieces and decorated in aquamarine. The effect was quite charming, with the delicate color giving a lift to the furniture. Tall narrow windows overlooked a formal garden, and Martha decided she faced out onto what might be called the front yard in a less pretentious home.

"Shall I unpack for you, miss?" Ruth asked, and Martha noticed that her suitcases were at the foot of the bed.

"Thank you, I'll take care of that."

Ruth turned to leave, hesitated, then said, "Mrs. Drew won't like your pants at the dinner table, miss."

"What? Oh—thanks for telling me, Ruth."

As the maid went out, Martha frantically reviewed her wardrobe. She had a long dress that would do, she thought, but she hesitated to wear it the first night at Black Tor. Otherwise, she'd packed almost all casual clothes—

pants, jeans, one uniform—just in case—and a dress that might be all right for shopping but might not do for the dinner table. Evidently at Black Tor one dressed for dinner, despite Jules's claim that the household was informal.

Martha unpacked, then glanced at her watch in dismay. Only three o'clock. What was she to do until dinner was served? Should she try to find Josephine? Thinking of the rambling house, she concluded that she probably couldn't find her. She sighed and sat on the bed, then finally stretched out on top of the coverlet.

Had she acted impulsively? Was her attraction to Jules what had influenced her to take the job despite its inauspicious beginning with the stuffed cat? She shook her head. Stuffed animals. The killer whale in the foyer, the black-and-white motif of the Garrards'....

Martha drifted. There was the sullen sea, not quite an ocean though the water was salt. Gray. Then the face, bearded, a black beard, curly, arrogant. No one she knew, and yet a haunting familiarity. A slash of white through the beard, like the streak in Jules's hair. Fear gripped Martha. She was unable to breathe, to speak. A weight sat on her chest.

"Hello."

She couldn't respond.

"Are you asleep?"

Martha opened her eyes and gazed into a childish face inches from her own. Hazel eyes stared into hers. She shook her head in confusion and tried to sit up.

CHAPTER THREE

"You're not an old lady," the little girl said.

Martha managed to shift the child's weight off her chest and sit up. She looked at the girl and was startled. A white wing of hair streaked the otherwise black curls.

"My name's Sarah. Yours is Martha, isn't it?"

Martha nodded, still examining the girl with interest. Whose child was she? Jules hadn't mentioned her. Obviously she was a Garrard. "How old are you, Sarah?" she inquired.

"I'm six." The hazel eyes regarded Martha thoughtfully. "I'm not supposed to ask you. Aunt Natalie says it's rude after you get grown up."

"Well, I don't mind telling you—I'm twenty-eight."

"Will I have to call you 'miss'? When Miss Eccles was here, she got mad if I didn't. Her first name was Clara, but hardly anyone could call her that."

"You may call me 'Martha.'"

Sarah smiled. "Miss Eccles was real old and her knees used to hurt and she couldn't climb up the stairs very good and Jo and me used to laugh but Aunt Natalie said that wasn't nice."

"Josephine?"

"I call her 'Jo,' but no one else can. She says that's her special name. I'm the only one who can ever call her that now."

"So you and Josephine are friends?"

"Sometimes. When she isn't mad at me. She gets mad easy. Are you going to get dressed up for dinner?"

Martha glanced at her watch. "Yes, I'd better change."

Sarah trailed her to the closet and watched while she extracted a simple blue sheath, the only street-length dress she'd brought. "I like blue," Sarah said. "Your eyes are pretty."

"Thank you. I think you're pretty, too. Ragged jeans and all."

Sarah grinned, her eyes lighting up. For a second Martha caught a fleeting resemblance to—whom? The cousin she'd met downstairs? But she couldn't pin it down, and then the feeling was gone.

"I don't get to eat in the dining room yet because Uncle Jules says children aren't civilized until they're twelve or older."

"He's your uncle?"

Sarah shrugged. "Aunt Natalie makes me call everyone 'aunt' or 'uncle.' She gets real mad if I forget. But I still say Jo when Aunt Natalie isn't there. She'll probably make me call you 'miss.' "

"Miss" because I'm not family, just a servant, Martha thought. *No "Aunt Martha" for a servant.* "It's 'Miss Jamison,' in case you have to," Martha told Sarah.

"You're nice. Will you be my friend?"

"I'd like to be friends." Who was this little girl who apparently didn't have a father or mother within the family here at Black Tor?

Martha found her necklace of silver and unpolished coral to wear with her blue sheath. This was as much as she could manage toward dressing up.

"Jo's coming," Sarah said.

Several minutes passed before there was a token knock at the door and Josephine pushed it open. Sarah must have unusually keen hearing.

"I see you've met Sarah," Josephine said. She looked at the little girl. "You'd better scoot."

Sarah went out without another word.

"She can be a nuisance," Josephine said. "But she's lonely."

"Doesn't she go to school?"

"No." Josephine frowned. "Cousin Louella acts as Sarah's tutor because she was a teacher before she came to live at Black Tor. But Louella's another old woman. This house reeks of age and death. Sometimes I can hardly stand it." She hit the gilt cage, and the canary swung back and forth crazily.

Martha said nothing.

"Look—about the tower. I—I really didn't know you weren't another of them—those grim old wardens Aunt Natalie's been foisting on me. I glanced out and saw Henry help you from the car and I just—well, I *had* to do something or burst. Did you ever feel you were coming to pieces, fragments showering around and about so that you'd never find them all and be whole again?"

"Yes," Martha said.

Josephine had been facing away from her, gazing out the window, but at that moment she swung around and faced Martha.

"You mean that, don't you?" She sighed. "Maybe you can understand, then." She moved closer to Martha. "Did Jules tell you about me? Did he tell you I was crazy because I believe in signs and omens? Did he tell you I tried to kill myself?"

"Well—not exactly like that."

Josephine turned her head and saw the silver-and-coral necklace on the dressing table. Picking it up, she ran the necklace through her fingers. "Coral is of the sea, and the sea is lucky for you," she intoned, her dark eyes fixed on Martha's. "But not for me. Death waits for me there somehow, someday."

Martha swallowed, willing herself not to show any emotion, though the words made her spine tingle.

"This necklace will act as an amulet for you because of your affinity for the sea," Josephine went on, "and also because a friend gave it to you. A gift is always more potent than what we buy for ourselves."

Ginetha gave me the coral necklace last Christmas, Martha thought. *She's the only real friend I've ever had. A good guess on Josephine's part—but only a guess, of course.* "I like to wear the necklace," she began, "but...."

"But you don't believe any of the rest of it—you think I'm crazy!"

"Because I don't believe anything you say to me doesn't make you crazy," Martha said. "I'm not—not versed in the occult and can't accept what you're telling me. Nothing more."

"Jules told you to watch me, I know he did. But I didn't try to kill myself. Sometimes I feel there's no use in living, but I'll wait for my death, not leap to meet it. I did almost die three times in the past year, that much is true."

"I—he merely told me I was to be your companion."

Josephine stared at her, not moving.

Martha tentatively extended a hand. "I wouldn't know how to be a—a warden, Josephine. It's presumptuous to say I'll be a friend, but I'll try to be a friendly companion."

When Josephine still made no move, Martha touched her arm gently, then withdrew her hand.

After a moment Josephine said, "I have to change for dinner." She nodded at Martha's bed, where the blue dress lay. "I see someone filled you in about Aunt Natalie."

"I'm afraid I didn't think of dressing for dinner when I packed," Martha said.

"Who does anymore? At least not all the time. But at Black Tor we might as well be back in the nineteenth century, as far as Natalie's notions go. You'll see." Josephine started for the door.

"Will you come back and show me where we're to dine? I'm not too sure of where I am in this house yet."

Josephine half smiled. "You never will be, either. I'm not, and I've lived here most of my life. But I'll show you where the dining room is, anyway. My bedroom's next to yours." She gestured.

A half-hour later, Josephine reappeared, wearing an ecru muslin dress that fell to the floor. Handmade lace frothed across the bodice and decorated the sleeves. Very simple, but Martha's practiced eye told her the dress was expensive.

She regretted that she hadn't chosen her own long dress, and thought wistfully of the clothes she'd rammed into boxes and put in storage with her other belongings when Ginetha descended on her in L.A. and insisted on helping her move out of the apartment and the lease money be damned. She could use some of those clothes at Black Tor.

As Martha and Josephine went into the corridor they passed a small white dog, and Martha almost bent to pet it, before she realized it was another stuffed pet.

"These halls are so gloomy," Josephine said. "All this dark paneling. The Victorians certainly loved wood—the darker the better."

Martha ran her fingers along the polished satiny panels. "But beautiful."

"I suppose so." Josephine didn't sound convinced. "I'll take you up to the tower tomorrow. Grandpa went wild with windows there, and it's like being in a different place, another house entirely."

Martha wondered dryly if the window Josephine had shattered would be repaired by then. Still, Josephine had apologized. But such a violent reaction! And she *could* have hurt someone.

As they descended the wide curving staircase, Martha thought the bold black and white of the killer whale was no less eye-catching from this angle. What a job to mount such a huge display!

"You're looking at *Orcinus orca*." Josephine's hand touched her temple. "I don't have the mark—it's usually the men who do."

Martha realized that Josephine was talking about the white streak in the Garrards' hair. "Sarah has one," she said.

"Oh, Sarah...."

"She's a Garrard isn't she?"

"I'm told so. Everyone is quite mysterious, trying to make you think that asking is in bad taste. Someone's by-blow, I suppose."

Martha frowned. Was Josephine telling her she didn't know where Sarah came from?

"Your brother has never married?"

"Jules?" Josephine glanced at Martha. "Oh, yes, years ago. She...died. I've often thought Sarah might be Jules's bastard. But he never lets on."

Josephine spoke casually, as though the subject were not very interesting. But, of course, if Sarah was six years old, everyone in the house must be used to her.

"Brace yourself," Josephine said as they crossed the foyer and entered a short hall. "Sherry with Aunt Natalie is out of another world."

Was this once the drawing room? Martha wondered as they came into a room with wainscotting lightened by pale yellow paper with a textured design. A Siamese cat crouched on the fireplace mantel, but Martha knew by now it wouldn't be a live cat.

Josephine led her to the sofa, where a large woman sat alone. Clearly in her sixties, she was clad in regal purple.

"This is Martha Jamison, Aunt Natalie," Josephine said.

For a moment Martha was overwhelmed by the woman's size and the piercing glare of the very dark eyes that looked into hers.

"Well, Miss Jamison. And do you consider yourself capable?"

Martha straightened her shoulders. Natalie Drew could be no more formidable than some of the charge nurses she'd encountered in the past. "How do you do, Mrs. Drew?" she replied. "I'm sure Mr. Garrard has discussed my credentials with you."

Natalie pressed her lips together. "Pieces of paper mean nothing."

"What I've done to earn those pieces of paper are my credentials, Mrs. Drew."

"Perhaps. We'll see."

"Would you care for some sherry?" Charn stood at her elbow, proffering a wineglass.

"Thank you." Martha took the thin-stemmed glass.

"Don't monopolize the girl, Aunt Nat," Charn said. "First nurse we've ever gotten in here under a hundred."

To Martha's surprise, Natalie gave Charn a wintry smile.

"Very well. Miss Jamison and I will speak another time."

Martha moved away with alacrity, evading Charn's attempt to pin her in a small alcove to the left of the beige marble fireplace. A gray-haired woman, tall and thin, wearing pince-nez, appeared in the doorway. She blinked at Martha in surprise.

"This is our new nurse, Louella," Charn said. "The wheel's finally turned up a winner."

Louella smiled nervously and darted past them before Martha could properly introduce herself. There was no sign of Jules or of Matthew Drew. Josephine had disappeared. Martha sipped at her sherry.

"Your freckles are charming," Charn said. "They give you a golden look."

Martha smiled politely. When she raised her eyes to meet his gaze, she was surprised to find him staring over her head. She turned and saw a short muscular man who glanced at her as he left the room. A servant?

Jules came in.

A bell tinkled and Natalie rose. Charn immediately left Martha to give his arm to her. Jules nodded at Martha but didn't offer his arm. She followed him across the short hall to the dining room.

Warm wood paneled the room entirely—floors, walls and ceiling. A cream-colored Oriental rug covered part of the parquet flooring, and portraits ringed the walls. The table was designed to seat at least fourteen and was now draped in immaculate white linen. Crystal water goblets sparkled in the light from an ornate chandelier of brass and cut glass.

Jules seated Martha, then moved quickly to help Louella into her chair. Charn was doing the same for Natalie when Josephine slipped into the room, her cheeks flushed. She slid into her chair and smoothed her hair with a quick motion. Everyone was seated when a white-haired man joined them.

He looks like the pictures I've seen of Harry Truman, Martha thought, *same size and everything.* She glanced from him to Natalie. Was this Matthew Drew? Younger and smaller than his wife, if so.

Jules sat at the head of the table, Natalie to his right, Matthew Drew to his left. Martha was next, then Josephine. Charn sat by Natalie, then came Louella.

Martha found herself directly across the table from Charn. He grinned at her and winked, and she smiled, then looked away, up at the portraits. She certainly didn't want Charn to think she was interested in him. The last thing she wanted was to become involved with a man in a household where she was a paid employee. It hadn't been appropriate in the age when the house had been built, and it wasn't appropriate now.

She found herself gazing at the face she'd seen in her dreams—a painting of a man's face, his black, arrogantly tilted beard streaked with white, his dark hair showing the Garrard mark. She stared, fascinated.

"What?" She'd alerted Charn, who turned in his chair to see what she was looking at. "Oh, that's old Abel. Quite a lad."

But how could she have dreamed of a man she'd never met, a man who'd been dead for years? Once more she seemed to see the gray sea in back of the face.

Then Natalie spoke, and the illusion faded. "We do not serve wine with our meals, Miss Jamison. I make this apologia should you be surprised at the omission. We are not teetotalers, but wine has never been served at a Garrard table."

Martha saw that she was not expected to comment.

The meal was excellent and deftly served by Ruth and an elderly manservant, whom Jules called Francis. Martha enjoyed the poached salmon despite the fact that she'd been gorging herself on salmon ever since she'd gotten to Seattle. She hadn't realized that fresh-caught fish could be so delicious. In Flagstaff, the only salmon she'd ever had was canned. And Southern California wasn't great salmon country, either.

Martha turned to Josephine. "I really like your salmon."

Josephine seemed dazed, and she'd hardly eaten anything. "What? Oh, salmon."

What was the matter with her? She'd been alert and talkative earlier. Where had she gone after introducing Martha to Aunt Natalie? Unease prickled along Martha's nerves. She was supposed to be looking after Josephine. She thought of Josephine's flushed face. Was she taking some drug? Was this at the root of her problems? Was drug overdosage what had brought her close to death those three times?

The eyes of the portrait seemed to stare at Martha. Abel Garrard's eyes. Hastily she looked away and met the nearly identical gaze of his grandson, Jules. If Jules grew a beard, would it be white streaked?

Unnerved, she turned her face toward Josephine again. The girl's head was bent; she was looking at something in her lap. Martha glanced down and caught a glimpse of bold green handwriting. "Dear Jo," she read, before Josephine crumpled the letter in her hand and shifted her position in the chair.

"Jo"? Sarah's words came back to her: "Her special name. I'm the only one who can ever call her that now."

What did the letter mean, then—someone from the past? What was Josephine's past?

The manservant, Francis, came into the dining room and spoke into Jules's ear. Martha saw Jules frown, then look her way. She tensed.

"You have a phone call, Martha," he said.

CHAPTER FOUR

THE TELEPHONE WAS SHUT AWAY in what amounted to a deluxe closet near the foyer.

"Martha?"

Not Ginetha's voice—a man's, vaguely familiar.

"Is this—this isn't Bran?"

"You sound shocked."

"But I—how did you know where I was?"

"I saw you get into that Rolls with the chauffeur and I asked a local, who told me who the car belonged to."

"Oh."

"I suppose you're wondering why I called."

"Yes. I was at dinner. . . ."

"I thought that maybe since you're staying on in Victoria—you are, aren't you?—you might like to sightsee with me sometime."

I didn't encourage him—I know I didn't, she told herself.

"And another thing," Bran went on. "I'll be coming to the house tomorrow. I—"

"Oh, no, I don't think you should do that. I've just—"

"Wait. I have business with Mr. Garrard. It's quite a co-incidence that you're staying there, and so I thought I'd call tonight—otherwise I probably wouldn't see you when I came."

"You won't, anyway," Martha said. "I'm—I work here. I'm not a guest."

"You work there?"

"Yes. I'm a nurse. Now, Bran, please, I must get back to the table. What will my employer think of—"

"A nurse!" Bran exclaimed, cutting her short.

"What's the matter with that?"

"Why, nothing. Only—I always think of nurses as granite blocks of authority. You're far too pretty to—"

"Don't be a chauvinist. But really, Bran, I can't—"

"You must be taking care of old Mr. Garrard."

"No, as a matter of fact I'm not. Goodbye, Bran."

"Wait. I really would like to see you again. . . ."

He was persistent, so he'd probably phone again. She didn't even know how Jules felt about her receiving personal calls on his time.

"Why don't you write me a note to let me know where you're staying," she said. "I could arrange to call you then if I have some free time. I really must hang up now, Bran. Goodbye." She set down the phone despite his protest.

Martha saw Natalie climbing the stairs as she came out of the alcove. Jules crossed the foyer, passing her. Obviously the family was no longer at dinner.

"Everything all right?" Jules asked.

"The call was personal, not necessary," she said. "I'm sorry. I'll try to see it doesn't happen again."

"Francis mentioned it was a local call," Jules said. "I didn't realize you knew anyone in Victoria."

"I don't—not really. But—well, there was someone on the ferry, and he found out where I was going." Damn Bran for his persistence!

"Oh—a young man."

She might as well tell Jules everything Bran had said; after all, he'd be there in person the following day, and she wouldn't put it past him to ask to see her. "I didn't expect him to call," she said. "But he—his name is Branwell Lowrey, and apparently he'll be seeing you on business tomorrow. . . ."

Jules frowned, then nodded. "Oh, yes. The museum, of course."

"He didn't realize I was here as an employee. I—we only had an impersonal conversation on the boat. I don't know why. . . ." She paused, annoyed and embarrassed at her position.

Juls smiled at her. "Don't be too hard on Dr. Lowrey, Martha. You're a most attractive young woman, and I certainly don't expect you to shut yourself away with Josephine seven days a week. We'll do something about arranging your free time tomorrow." He moved away.

"Dr." Lowrey? she mused as she started up the stairs. Bran, a doctor? Of what? Jules had mentioned a museum. Here she'd thought Bran was a carefree backpacker. . . .

And Jules considered her attractive. She smiled to herself.

Martha hesitated in the corridor outside her room. Should she tap at Josephine's door? How close a supervision did Jules expect? She really must insist on talking to Josephine's doctor soon, because apparently no one there was going to tell her the exact nature of the girl's problem. She rapped lightly. "Josephine?"

There was a click. Had the door been locked? Was a lock wise with someone who may have tried to kill herself? Then the door opened. Josephine's face was pale and her eyes were haunted.

"Do you feel ill?" Martha asked.

"Martha. . . ." Josephine stepped back and motioned her in, closing and, yes, locking the door behind her. "Oh, Martha, I wish I could trust you."

"Trust me?"

"But you'll tell Jules, won't you? Like those others reported everything to Aunt Natalie. And Jules is against me like all the rest."

"I might not have to tell Jules. However, I am going to

talk to your doctor, and I don't think I should keep any-thing from him.''

To her surprise, Josephine gave a sigh of relief. ''Oh, Dr. Marston. I don't think you'd need to tell him, not at all. It's not—not about the time I was so—so sick. This is from before. But I'm afraid, I don't understand and there's no one I can trust. Except—'' Her large yellow eyes stared at Martha. ''They told you, didn't they? That I was somewhere else when I was seventeen. And eighteen. I was there two years. And I—just don't remember about that time. The two years are all blurred, fogged over.''

''But that's not what frightens you now?''

Josephine shook her head. ''You saw that note at the table, didn't you? Did you tell?''

Martha remembered the green writing. '' 'Dear Jo,' '' she said aloud. ''No, I didn't say anything about it. Why should I?''

''You're here as a spy, you know. Didn't Jules tell you?''

''I'm here as a companion. I'm a nurse, not a spy, Jose-phine.''

''The note is from someone. Oh, Martha, he's dead. How can he write me a letter? Am I going mad, really mad? I'm so afraid.''

''Where did the note come from? The mail?''

''I never get mail—they'd open it if I did. No, Sarah mo-tioned me out of the parlor before dinner and slipped the note into my hand. I asked her where she got it, and she said that Bill Wong—he's one of the gardeners—gave the envelope to her when she was playing outside and told her it was for Miss Josephine.''

''It's not from this—Bill Wong?''

''Oh, no.''

''Would you let me read it?''

Josephine opened a book lying on her bedside stand and extracted a crumpled piece of paper.

"Dear Jo," Martha read in the bold green handwriting. "I haven't forgotten. Love, Diego." "'Diego'?" she said to Josephine.

"I called him that. He called me 'Jo.' I never knew his name. He didn't know mine." Josephine sat on her bed, staring down at the paper Martha had returned to her. "I was sixteen, but he didn't know that, either, because I told him I was older. We truly loved each other, but he died—he drowned when the boat foundered. How can he write me now?"

"He drowned when you were sixteen?"

Tears filled Josephine's eyes. "Yes. I went to the docks to see him, and I found out his boat—he worked on a salmon boat." She began to cry.

Martha sat beside her and put an arm around her shoulders. *Johann's dead, too,* she thought, *but my tears are all shed. . . they were shed long before his death.*

"You don't know," Josephine sobbed. "No one knows."

"My—my husband died," Martha told her softly. "I can understand." She handed tissues to Josephine.

Josephine mopped at her face and sat up straighter. Martha dropped her arm but continued to sit next to her.

"I didn't know you'd been married."

"Now you have a secret to keep," Martha said. "I didn't tell your brother. I use my maiden name now, so I didn't think it mattered."

"I only knew Diego three days," Josephine said.

"Here in Victoria?"

"Oh, no. Aunt Natalie was too strict. I—there was a friend from school whose family moved to Seattle, and she invited three of her girlfriends from Victoria to a weekend birthday party. I was one of the girls. We went over on the evening ferry and were to come back by plane. Her parents were meeting us at the dock." Josephine smiled faintly. "I was very excited, because I had so many restrictions that a trip unchaperoned was an event. Not alone, really, but girls my age didn't count.''

"This was when you were sixteen?''

Josephine nodded. "The other two girls were what we called best friends, and I was the third wheel, rather. So I went onto the deck even though it was foggy and cold. Wanting to savor my freedom, I imagine. And—he was there. Diego.''

"Was he Spanish?''

"I don't know. We met in the fog and we didn't talk about who we were. I found out he worked the salmon boats out of Seattle and had been to the island for a day of sightseeing. He liked Victoria. He found out I was going to visit a friend in Seattle. I lied and said I was through school because I thought he might think I was just a kid otherwise. We knew there was something between us and he kissed me, and nothing like that had ever happened to me before.'' Josephine gently touched the note that lay beside her on the bed. "Nothing has since.''

"You never saw him again?''

"Only twice more. His boat was in because of the nets—something wrong with the nets. He was from San Diego. He'd worked on the tuna seiners down there. I remember every word he ever said to me.

"He met me in a park near the house where I was staying. He told me what time he'd be there, and I sneaked out and met him. We fell in love. He said he'd come and see me in Victoria, but I wouldn't tell him who I was—I couldn't. He'd find out I was sixteen, and anyway, Aunt Natalie would never let us be together. He was older—he said he was twenty-one—and he worked on the boats. She'd have been horrified.''

Josephine looked at Martha. "I didn't know what to do. I was going home the next day, and I'd never see him again and I couldn't stand it. So that night I—I waited until everyone was asleep and I crept out of the house and took a bus to the docks. I knew Diego was staying on the boat, so I went to find him. But other men were there with him, and they were having a party and drinking wine, and they laughed when I came by and they teased Diego, and I had some of the wine because it was foggy and cold...." Josephine looked away from Martha and gripped her hands in her lap.

"Did your friend's parents find you were missing?"

"No. But the next morning I was too sick to fly home and a doctor had to come to their house and give me shots for three days. Then he said maybe I should take the ferry back with a stateroom to rest in instead of flying, because of the danger of middle-ear infection.

"So I managed to get to the dock once more, and that's when I heard about Diego's boat sinking. I ran away from the—from my friend's parents—and I found where I'd been the night with Diego, and one of the men from the party was there working on another boat, and when he saw me he came down and told me Diego had been drowned. I guess he must've taken me back to the ferry, only I don't remember. Because I did get back to Victoria, but I had a relapse and had to go to St. Joe's with pneumonia. I know I came home from the hospital, but after that things go dimmer and dimmer until I don't remember anything...."

"And you never told anyone about Diego?"

"No."

"Not even Dr. Marston?"

"It wasn't his business. He wouldn't understand."

Martha looked at Josephine's bent head. She felt an ache in her throat for the teenage romance that had somehow led the girl into a mental breakdown. Had she been unstable prior to meeting Diego? Diego, who evidently wasn't dead. Why had it taken him so long to get in touch? "Is the note in his handwriting?" she asked Josephine.

"I—I don't know. I never saw his handwriting. But who else would know?"

"If the letter's from Diego, obviously he's alive, Josephine. The dead don't write notes."

"I know, but I'm afraid." Josephine glanced wildly around the room, and Martha thought of a caged bird suddenly offered a way out but too frightened to leave the well-known cage.

"If this isn't a hoax, he'll get in touch with you again. You were right to share the note with me."

"You won't tell. You promised me."

"Well, for now, no. But we don't know enough yet, not even if this really is from Diego." *Or what he wants after all these years if it is,* Martha finished, but she didn't say it aloud. Another thought crept in: could Josephine have written the note to herself? *I'll have to talk to Sarah,* Martha decided, *and this Bill Wong.*

Later, in her own bed, Martha went over what Josephine had told her. The note seemed quite odd. If this was the long-lost Diego who had finally found his love, why wouldn't he march up to the door and ask for Josephine?

Martha drifted into sleep, her mind a confused jumble of thoughts. She awakened with a start, opening her eyes to darkness. Had someone called her name? Did Josephine need her?

She had started to swing her legs over the edge of the bed when someone sat down next to her. "Josephine?" she asked.

To her horror, a hand slid across her breast, caught at her shoulder and pushed her back down on the bed. She struggled to free herself, knowing this was a man, for she felt a man's strength in the hands.

"Let me go!" she managed, before a mouth came down on hers, stopping her words, her breath.

She moaned in fright and desperation.

CHAPTER FIVE

"I KNOW WHO YOU ARE, Marty Collier. Don't fight, no use to fight." The man spoke in a husky whisper directly into her ear. "Don't pretend with me," he said.

Martha froze. Then, as his hand slid the length of her body, she jerked her head away and screamed. His grip loosened, and she sat upright to reach for the bedside lamp, but even as she did so her door opened and closed so swiftly she barely saw a dark outline.

She switched on the light. Her room was empty. She stared at the closed door. She hadn't imagined it. There'd been a man there who had called her Marty Collier and tried to—expected her to. . . .

The doorknob turned and Martha gasped, shrinking back on the bed. The door opened slowly and Josephine's face appeared. "Did you call me?"

"Oh, Josephine, someone was in here!"

Josephine came into the room and shut the door. "Who?"

Belatedly Martha wondered at the wisdom of telling her.

"Who was in your room?" Josephine repeated.

"I—I don't know. A man. He—threatened me."

"What did he do?"

Was Josephine's glance too knowing, her eyes too bright?

"Did he try to rape you?" Josephine demanded. "Is that why you screamed? I heard you, but I wasn't sure. I thought maybe I'd been the one to call out, like I do when I have nightmares, but it didn't seem as if I had."

"I screamed," Martha acknowledged. "He—frightened me."

"Who was it?"

"I told you—I don't know. A man."

Josephine came over and sat on the edge of the bed. "Well, then it was either Charn or Jules. Unless it was one of the servants. But I can't see Henry or Francis. . . ." She giggled. "And Simon stays with daddy all the time."

"Could some stranger have gotten into the house?" Martha asked, remembering the whisper that told her he knew she was Marty. . . no use to pretend. Who knew of her past?

Josephine shrugged. "I don't know who you might have following you around," she said. "In fact, I don't know anything about you." Her tone was accusing. "I told you all about me, but you hardly said one word about yourself."

"No one's following me," Martha said. But would Charn or Jules come into her room as the man had?

"Have you been a nurse all your life?" Josephine asked. "You're pretty. . . ."

Martha had no intention of talking about her past. "It's late," she said. "Thanks for coming in. I was frightened, but I'll lock the door now. I should have before, but I didn't think. . . ."

"I always do," Josephine said. "You'd better too, in this house."

Martha locked the door after letting Josephine out. She lay awake afterward, thinking of Johann Collier. There'd been headlines in the California papers. After all, Johann was famous in his way. He'd written the script for and then directed *The Unmasking of Hell*, which had turned out to be the most controversial film of that year. "Genius or madman?" the papers had asked afterward. Neither, she thought sadly. A man driven beyond his own limits by circumstance and by his own frightening urges.

Marty Collier. She'd been in the headlines at the end. Who in Victoria knew that Martha Jamison was Marty Collier?

She wasn't the woman Johann had pictured so vividly in the movie script and who had been played so sensuously by Maria Canyon, unknown before her starring role as Nida in *The Unmasking of Hell*. Johann had come to confuse Maria with his creation, and Maria was anything but a woman driven to sexual excess by her own neuroses. Maria was, instead, a capable actress.

Poor Johann. For she, his wife, hadn't been Nida, either. No woman could have been. After he'd seen his creation take flesh, so to speak, in the movie, he'd been forced past his limits into the trackless realm that lies beyond. Not really insanity—just uncharted space that frightened him into destruction.

Latent schizophrenia, the doctor had said. She remembered Johann laughing when he told her. The psychiatrist, Dr. Towers, the very eminent Frederic Towers. Shrink, Johann had called him. Headshrinker—no better than a witch doctor, Johann had insisted. Was it because Johann was afraid of discovering what dwelt in his own mind? Of course the newspapers quoted Dr. Towers at great length afterward.

If only there'd been a way to buy time for Johann. A place where there was no pressure. Her love had shifted from passion to fierce protectiveness. She'd tried to mother him and he'd hated it. But she'd felt responsible; no one else seemed to understand his fragility. Until the end she hadn't really understood that no one can take responsibility for another adult.

And now someone at Black Tor knew her as the Marty Collier the papers had pictured—a Nida, insatiable, hopelessly neurotic. She wasn't; she never had been. Any more than Maria Canyon was Nida.

"I don't know how you managed," Maria told her the one time they'd met after Johann's death. "He was a man obsessed. I could hide from him when I had to. But you...." Maria paused and stared hard at Marty. "You were forced to play Nida."

Marty shook her head. "No. Never that."

"Forced to *be* Nida, then, if only in his mind," Maria had insisted. "Johann was mad, of course. Quite mad."

Marty couldn't answer, recalling the last ugly scene. She'd fled from Johann by locking herself in the bathroom, where there was an inner bolt, put there at Johann's order to protect himself from anyone entering while he was caring for his body. At the last, the bolt had protected her from Johann. Would he have killed her as he'd threatened?

She'd seen him use the knife hundreds of times to open letters—a Thai dagger, actually, with an alien god carved into the handle. But this time he'd used it on her, cutting her arm and breast before she gained the sanctuary of the bathroom. She'd huddled naked inside the bathroom, blood dripping on the pink tile, too distraught to do more than listen to Johann screaming curses in the bedroom. He'd splintered the bottom of the door by repeated kicking, before the phone distracted him. Ringing on and on, a shrill accompaniment to his ravings.

Finally he answered the phone—she knew because that's where she found him when the long silence gave her courage to wrap a towel around herself and venture out of the bathroom. Johann lay sprawled by the bed, phone still clutched in his hand, the dagger plunged into his chest.

The papers had played up the death for all it was worth, drawing parallels between Johann's death and *The Unmasking of Hell* with its overtones of the occult. Even the phone call was referred to as "mysterious," since no one admitted to having called Johann. Dr. Towers was quoted out of context to bolster the articles. Only Dr. Towers's testimony had kept her from being accused of murder. The papers had liked that, too. Nida was a woman who drove men mad—drove them to destruction.

But she wasn't Nida.

And she was no longer Marty Collier, either. She was Martha Jamison, just as if Johann had never existed.

Despite the locked door, she slept fitfully, waking to dawn and an insistent tapping. Who was at the door?

Martha wrapped herself in her robe and padded over to ask.

"It's me. You locked me out." A child's voice. Sarah.

"Are you going to be like Jo, always locking your door?" Sarah demanded when Martha let her in. "I thought you'd be different."

"Why are you up so early?" Martha asked.

"Because I'm going to spend my money. If you and Jo ask Henry to take you into town, I can go, too. Will you?"

"You'll have to talk to Josephine."

"Oh, she'll go if you want to. She likes you. I want to go today. I don't ever get any money to spend."

"But you have money now?"

"The man gave money to Bill and he gave me some. Bill's nice. He can sound like all different kinds of birds, and he's Jimmy's grandfather and—"

"What man?" Martha broke in, remembering Josephine's note.

"I don't know—just a man. I saw him talking to Bill. Jo told me not to tell about the paper, but she showed you, I bet."

Martha watched the girl as she wandered about the bedroom, picking up a traveling clock here, a lipstick there. The white wing of hair that looked so natural on Jules seemed out of place on this child, somehow shadowing the innocence of her face.

"Will you ask Henry?"

Martha thought of her phone call the day before during dinner. She'd rather not be in the house when Bran came to talk to Jules. She wasn't sure if she wanted to see him again, for there had been nothing between them as far as she was concerned. He was pleasant enough, but....

"I'll talk to Josephine," Martha told Sarah. "Maybe she'd like an outing."

After the girl left, Martha relocked the door and showered, dressing in a casual costume of brown pants with a pale orange shirt. The sun was high enough that she felt she could knock on Josephine's door.

Josephine was reading in bed. Martha glanced at the book title. *Growing Pains*, by Emily Carr.

"She was persecuted by this town, actually persecuted," Josephine said angrily. She gestured at the book. "I'm reading her autobiography. They said her paintings were ridiculous and she was crazy. They drove her away even though she loved the island. Why are people like that?"

"I'm afraid I don't know who Emily Carr is," Martha said.

"Oh, that's right. You're not Canadian. She was a painter, and now everyone knows how good she really was. But then, when she was alive...." Josephine shook her head. "I understand how helpless she felt. They thought she was mad because she liked Indians and even lived with Indian families and shared their way of life and painted them and the forests and what was wild and natural. Women didn't do that in Emily's time. She stayed free, though. They wounded her, but they never captured her and put her in a cage."

"She sounds interesting. I'd like to see her paintings."

"Oh, would you really? There're some prints in her old family house in town, and the art gallery on Moss Street has originals. I'll ask Henry if he'll take us in. Of course he'll have to ask Jules if it's all right, but I pretend not to know that. I hate to be dependent on Jules! When daddy dies—'' She broke off. ''You think I'm awful. But my father didn't want me in the first place. He married my mother because she was young and pretty. He wanted her—not me. She wasn't well after I was born, and she died when I was three. Aunt Natalie moved into Black Tor after that.''

''Was your aunt married then?''

''No. Uncle Matthew was an—afterthought. He's—'' Josephine stopped. ''Well, he doesn't count.''

''Your father's quite ill?''

''He's dying. And when he does, I'll have my own money.'' Josephine frowned and was silent a moment. Then she kicked the covers aside and got out of bed. ''Jules and Aunt Natalie will find a way to keep me from getting the money. That's why they want everyone to think I'm crazy.'' She glared at Martha.

''Well, I haven't even seen your doctor yet,. much less talk to him,'' Martha said. ''No one's told me you're—''

''They don't *say* it,'' Josephine broke in. ''They hint. 'She tried to kill herself,' they say. I've never tried to do such a thing.''

''Are you telling me you think someone else was responsible for your so-called suicide attempts?''

Josephine nodded impatiently. ''Yes, of course. I don't know if they really wanted me to die or just to seem crazy. But I lock my door now. I'm careful.''

Martha's thoughts jumbled together in a kaleidoscope of speculation. Paranoid ideation? Or could Josephine possibly be right? What did her doctor think? How did this man from her past, the man called ''Diego,'' fit in?

''Did you sleep all right after what happened last night?'' Josephine asked.

Martha nodded, reluctant to think about it.

"I can't imagine who the man was," Josephine said. "Although Jules *has* been different since Cynthia was killed six years ago. I don't think there's been any women who've interested him since then."

" 'Cynthia'?"

"Jules's wife." Josephine began pulling clothes from the closet and discarding them in disgust. "I don't have anything to wear," she moaned.

Martha picked a shocking-pink ensemble from the floor. "This looks charming," she said. "The color must be striking on you."

"But it's old," Josephine wailed. "All my clothes are old. I haven't been shopping in months. I didn't care—" She stopped and smiled at Martha. "Now it's different, now that I know Diego's alive." Josephine suddenly threw her arms in the air and twirled in a circle. "I wouldn't let myself think about him in case—in case...." She paused, taking a deep breath and then sighing. "But it has to be true. I'll see him again." She looked anxiously at Martha. "Will he still love me? Am I pretty? It's been so long since I cared. My hair...." She lifted a strand, let it drop, then gestured at the clothes strewn about the floor. "I must be—like I was. But I—I can't remember." Her eyes filled with tears.

"Wear the pink," Martha said, making her voice positive. "With your coloring it's just right. And you're very pretty—no one could think otherwise." *Should I tell Jules about Diego's letter?* she asked herself. *What's my duty to my employer? But if I tell him, I'll lose Josephine's trust. Perhaps I can watch her carefully for any other attempts by this Diego—if it is Diego—to get in touch with her. If I feel she's threatened in any way, even by her own feelings, then I can let Jules know.*

Martha watched the radiance return to Josephine's face as she gathered up the pink outfit and looked at herself in the mirror. "The color does make me look nice, doesn't it?"

"Lovely."

I'll call Dr. Marston today, Martha told herself. *He may be able to help me decide what's safe for Josephine. And I must know what his diagnosis is before I become too involved in what she tells me and what her relatives tell me. I need a doctor's appraisal.*

A cold sliver seemed to be lodged in her mind, chilling as it irritated. The night before. Who knew she was Marty Collier? Who had tried to force her to intimacies, believing that she would welcome them? Jules? Charn? An unknown man, someone she couldn't even imagine? Surely it hadn't been Bran—how could he have gotten into the house? She thrust away the thoughts.

"Instead of you talking to Henry," Martha said, "I think I'd better ask Jules if we can go into Victoria today. He may have something else he wants me to do."

"Oh, all right," Josephine replied. "I suppose you must."

No one was at the table when they went down to breakfast, but Charn came in after they'd been served. "Quite an early start this morning," he said.

"You mean, for me or for you?" Josephine countered, smiling at him.

"Both of us. Maybe Martha will prove to be a good influence." He smiled back at them.

Martha looked into his clear blue eyes and wondered if he could possibly have been the man in her room the previous night.

Later, talking to Jules in the library, she asked herself the same question. How could either of the men have confronted her so openly that morning if they were guilty?

"I think Josephine would enjoy a trip to Victoria," Jules said. "As a matter of fact, I believe I'll join you.

We'll go after lunch, perhaps have tea in the Empress Hotel. I haven't been in years. It's a touristy thing to do, but it's rather fun.''

Jules didn't look like a man who ever did touristy things. Nor did he seem a man who would invade her room. His dark eyes were reserved, even wary.

"Sarah mentioned she'd like to come along," Martha said.

A crease appeared between Jules's brows.

"I think she wants to buy something," Martha added.

"I imagine she can stay with Henry, then," Jules said. "I don't know that the art gallery or tea at the hotel would interest her."

Did having the child with him in public make him uncomfortable? Martha wondered. For the first time, the significance of Josephine's remark about Jules's wife's death struck her. Six years earlier, Josephine had said. Cynthia had died six years earlier. And Sarah was six. Had Jules been having an illicit affair while his wife was still alive? With Sarah as the result?

"You can tell your friend he's quite mistaken if he thinks I can be manipulated into giving up the whale," Jules said suddenly. "Now that I've had time to consider the coincidence, I wonder if you haven't arrived here wearing false colors."

CHAPTER SIX

MARTHA STARED BLANKLY at Jules. What was he talking about?

"Your phone call at dinner last night, the same man coming to see me from the museum today. You say you 'happened' to meet on the ferry. I doubt the coincidence."

"If you're referring to Bran Lowrey, I can assure you I've told you the truth." She raised her chin. "I'll submit my resignation anytime you wish."

He waved his hand. "No, no. I need you here, since you *are* a nurse—I've checked out your credentials. If I find I'm wrong about the conspiracy, you'll have my apologies." His voice held an edge of mockery.

What an arrogant man! she thought, furious. "If I'm to stay, I do have a request," she told him, keeping her voice steady with effort. "I'd like to talk to Dr. Marston about Josephine—today, if possible."

Jules frowned. "Why the hurry?" he asked.

"Because I must hear the doctor's version of Josephine's problems before I can be sure of myself with her."

"That could wait."

Martha eyed him coldly. "I'm afraid I must insist."

He shrugged again. "Very well. I'll give you his number."

"Thank you." Head held high, she marched from the room. Passing through the foyer, she glanced upward at the leaping killer whale. How could it be connected with her or Bran? She stopped, feeling heat in her cheeks. Had

Bran deliberately introduced himself to her on the boat, knowing she was coming to Black Tor?

But then she relaxed and started up the stairs. He couldn't have known she was—there was no way for him to have found out. She wasn't much for coincidence, but that's all their meeting could have been. He *had* seen her get into the Rolls, however, and that explained his continued interest in her, despite her lack of encouragement.

At least the accusation from Jules, humiliating as it was, had warned her of Bran's motives. She'd certainly not see him again. If only Jules didn't intend to come with them that day, Martha thought, although she recognized the wisdom of his being along. She didn't yet know enough about Josephine.

Josephine accepted the fact of Jules's joining them with resignation. "I told you he spies on me," was all she said.

Martha called Dr. Marston before noon. "So you're Josephine's new companion," he said. "A psychiatric nurse, I hear. Very fine. The girl needs someone her age, but a capable someone."

"Doctor, I'd like to talk to you about her past history."

"And I'd like to talk to you, too, Miss Jamison. Jules tells me you'll be in town today. Why don't you drop by around three?"

"Yes, of course, doctor. Thank you."

So, after visiting the art gallery, Martha went to Dr. Marston's office while Henry drove Jules, Sarah and Josephine to shop.

Dr. Marston was about fifty, with wavy chestnut hair barely touched with gray. He wore tweed, and a pipe lay on his desk. Chestnut eyes confronted her through rimless glasses. *Not mod at all,* she thought. *Quite English, really.* His diplomas delineated his progress from medical school through internship and psychiatric residency and testified to his membership in the proper medical societies.

"Ah, yes, quite pretty, too, I see. Josephine is fortunate."

Martha smiled tentatively. "I like Josephine," she said. "But I get varying stories from those around her."

Dr. Marston nodded, then leaned back in his chair and steepled his hands, patting the fingertips together lightly. "I didn't see Josephine Garrard as a patient until she was nineteen years old. At that time, she'd returned from the States and was living once again at Black Tor. She'd been home for some time but hadn't been eating well. Norman Garrard, her father, called and asked me to see her. I suggested their family physician, but Norman insisted on me. I found the girl depressed, with some evidence of having experienced an amnesiac state for the previous two years. She seemed to have no idea what had happened to her in that time." Dr. Marston brought his chair upright and rested his elbows on the desk. "I was reluctant to stay on the case."

"Why?" Martha asked.

"Lack of information. Deliberate concealment. I've never been told where Josephine stayed during those two years in the States. Was she in an institution for the mentally ill? I don't know. Norman isn't talking, and Josephine honestly doesn't know."

"But you're her doctor at present?"

Dr. Marston took off his glasses and polished them. "Only because of my long friendship with the Garrard family." He sighed. "Well, Josephine gradually emerged from her depression, her appetite improved, and although she was reluctant to leave the house, I felt quite optimistic about her future. Until last year." He leaned forward, holding her eyes with his. "You must be very careful of possible suicide attempts, Miss Jamison. There've been three in this past year. An overdose of drugs twice and a fall."

"A fall?"

"Josephine may tell you she was pushed. But. . . ." He sighed again and picked up his pipe. "She apparently tried to throw herself off the cliff near the house. Her clothes caught on a bush, and one of the gardeners found her and managed to rescue her. She was unconscious from a head injury—a mild concussion, from which she recovered. That was the first. The next time, she tried drugs, and the little girl found her and alerted the nurse they had then. I believe she was the one before the woman you replaced."

"How many nurses has Josephine had?"

Dr. Marston thought for a moment. "Five that I know of. All older women, until now. I think the change to someone Josephine's age is an excellent idea."

"And the last suicide attempt?"

"Drugs again. I thought she'd stopped taking them and they'd been tossed out, but evidently not. This time she had a change of heart afterward and managed to crawl from her bed to the window and throw something through the glass. One of the servants heard the glass shatter."

The gardener again? Martha wondered. This Bill Wong who handled the mysterious note?

"Josephine denies that she took any drugs knowingly," Dr. Marston went on, "as I'm sure she told you. But you must remember that she's recovering from a depression, and you know, of course, that's the dangerous time for suicide attempts—during the recovery period."

Martha nodded.

"I've been at a loss to treat whatever pathology underlies the depression," he said. "Josephine hasn't divulged much material except for her feeling of desertion when her mother died, her overall feeling of being unwanted in the household, of being unloved. Those two missing years remain obstinately locked away—to Josephine as well as to me."

"But—Mr. Garrard must know, Josephine's father. Or her aunt, Mrs. Drew."

"As I've told you, Miss Jamison, I've been hampered by their refusal to tell me. All the same, I believed until last year that Josephine might recover enough to resume a fairly normal life. Now, of course, my prognosis is more guarded. She seems to have persecution feelings, thinks everyone is watching her." He nodded slowly. "To some extent she's right—we don't want her to try to take her life again."

"But, doctor, she locks her door at night—anything could happen and I wouldn't be able to get in," Martha exclaimed.

"The locked door was my idea," Dr. Marston said. "An attempt to allay her notion of being spied on. Jules has an extra key, of course. I'm surprised he hasn't told you. But there's some arrangement whereby you can look into her room from the one next door. Your bedroom, I would imagine."

Martha stared at the doctor. Why hadn't anyone told her?

"Is she psychotic, then?" she asked.

Dr. Marston frowned. "Without those two years. . . ." He paused. "On the basis of what I've seen—no. But there's always the question: did she have a schizophrenic break at sixteen? She shows certain indications that that might have been the case, but there's not enough for me to be sure."

Martha's mind whirred with conjecture as she watched Dr. Marston load his pipe from a humidor on his desk. Should she tell him about Diego? Maybe it was all a fantasy on Josephine's part. Still—there was the note. Unless Josephine had somehow arranged with this gardener to pretend to deliver a note to— No, wait—Sarah had mentioned seeing a man. If the note was genuine, then maybe

Diego was, too. She should tell someone, and Dr. Marston seemed to be the logical person.

Suddenly the receptionist came in to inform the doctor that a patient was waiting to see him.

"Will you excuse me, Miss Jamison?" he asked.

"Doctor, I think I should tell you—"

"We'll make another appointment in a month—I'd like to have your view of Josephine as you come to know her. Good day." He left the room.

Martha shrugged. She could always call him if this Diego business came to anything.

She left Dr. Marston's office and began walking down Douglas Street toward the Empress Hotel, where she was to meet the others in the lobby at four o'clock. She could see the huge turreted building as she approached, and soon she was close enough to make out every tiny balcony, tower and chimney, many seemingly stuck on for no reason. Ivy clung to the weathered brick. How many stories— five, six? Tea and crumpets in the lobby. She'd never had crumpets. What were they, anyway?

They'd never been to England, she and Johann. The money rolled in and the money rolled out; Johann spent whatever he made, and she didn't work for those four years—he laughed when she mentioned working. Still, there'd been more money than she'd dreamed of or even wanted, though Johann was never satisfied. They made impulsive trips to Acapulco and Hawaii, to the Caribbean, and to Las Vegas for Johann's gambling. But not to England. No crumpets.

Nor was Martha to taste a crumpet that day. As she approached the hotel entrance, she saw Henry's gray uniform barring her way. "Pardon me, miss, but Mr. Jules would like you to come to the car. It's this way, miss."

"Is Josephine all right, Henry?"

"As far as I know, miss."

Henry seated her in the back with Jules and Josephine. Sarah didn't raise her head from the comic book in which she was engrossed.

"I'm sorry to postpone tea at the Empress," Jules said. "We're going back to the house."

"That's quite all right," Martha said. She glanced at Josephine, who sat in the middle, and saw a smile quivering on her lips. Three suicide attempts? Martha thought. Josephine's pale skin was slightly flushed and she looked lovely. She looked—happy.

"The museum is over there," Jules pointed out as Henry turned a corner. "We're quite proud of this whole complex—bell tower, museum and community center. All new, and yet integrated architecturally."

Martha found it attractive and said so, all the time wondering if Jules were mocking her, referring in some way to her supposed conspiracy with Branwell Lowrey.

"Jules is mad at me," Josephine said.

He flashed his sister a malevolent look.

"He thinks I tried to run away." Josephine laughed. "I really didn't."

"We'll discuss the matter later," Jules said curtly.

"Oh, don't be such a stick." Josephine's voice was light. "Henry and Sarah are perfectly aware of what's going on."

Jules clenched his jaw, and Martha could see the muscles bunch together in his face. She turned away.

"I thought I saw someone I knew, so I ran out of the store to say hello, and Jules. . . ." Josephine turned up her hands and shrugged. "He thought I was escaping—isn't that the word, Jules?"

"This is neither the time nor the place for—"

Josephine laughed, and Jules stopped abruptly, reaching over and grasping his sister's arm above the elbow. "That's quite enough," he said. "You're not a child to indulge yourself at others' expense."

Martha saw how his fingers dug in, but Josephine gave no sign that he was hurting her. "Oh," she said, "excuse me, dear *kind* brother Jules."

He let her go and turned his head away. There was no more conversation during the drive back.

When they reached the house, Josephine hurried inside and ran up the stairs. Martha would have followed her, but Jules held her back. "You'll have to watch her closely," he said. "No trips to town. She tried to evade me in the store—deliberately. And this nonsense about seeing someone she knew—Josephine's been back home for four years and she's never tried to contact anyone. In fact, she's refused to see former friends when they've called here."

"I'll be careful," Martha said. "But are you sure she didn't catch sight of someone from—from the past? She—"

"Don't let her fool you, Martha. Josephine can be extremely devious. I assure you, she was trying to get away from me."

"But why?"

"I'm sure Dr. Marston spoke of the suicide attempts. How do I know what went through her head today? My theory is, she wanted to find a drug source."

"Has she been taking drugs without the doctor's advice?"

"I don't think she has lately." Jules frowned. "I can't be sure. She was addicted to barbiturates when she... came home. Dr. Marston advised a slow withdrawal to prevent serious physical problems, and we all believed it was working, until Josephine tried to kill herself. She must have been hiding them all along."

Why hadn't the doctor come right out and said that? Martha wondered. Everyone seemed to speak partial truths.

CHAPTER SEVEN

"Jo said she was going to hang her hair out the window. She said she'd been shut up in the tower too long," Sarah told them. "Does she mean like Rapunzel in the story? Because her hair isn't long enough, and besides, it's not golden."

"We'd better go up there," Jules stated.

"Why not let me go alone?" Martha asked.

Jules stared at her for a moment.

"What good am I to you if you won't allow me any responsibility?" she asked.

"I wish I could be—sure of you," he said.

"I think you should stay away from Josephine for the rest of the day," Martha told him. "You might provoke her where I wouldn't, since she has nothing to prove to me."

Jules sighed. "You may be right." His eyes hadn't left hers, and she felt almost mesmerized by his gaze. Such dark eyes, like the magic fairy-tale pool in the woodland, that dark bottomless pool luring the unwary to enchantment and death. . . .

Martha straightened her shoulders and turned away from Jules. "How do I climb to the tower?" she asked.

The door was down the hall from Josephine's room. Jules opened it. A spiral staircase wound up to another level between walls of dark wood paneling. Two small round windows of stained glass cast an amber gloom.

Jules saw her momentary pause. "I loved the tower when I was young," he said. "Now. . . ." He shrugged.

"But Josephine clings to being a child." Then, taking Martha's arm, he led her to the spiral steps. The door closed behind them. It was like being in a topaz cave. Jules pointed upward. "You won't find her on the next level— there's a door to the attics there—but don't stop climbing until you reach the top." His voice was low.

Martha nodded, somewhat intimidated by the prospect of a two-story climb up this twilight tower toward her enigmatic charge. She put her foot on the first step.

"Martha." Jules's voice was soft.

She looked at him.

"Forgive my suspicious nature," he said. His fingers brushed along her cheek. Then he turned and went out of the tower.

Martha began to climb, firmly pushing away the excitement of his touch. She came through the center opening into the second level and noticed two diamond-shaped windows where light filtered through green glass. A door was set into the wall on her left. She resumed the climb. *It's like being underwater,* she thought. She found the notion unpleasant. Her breathing quickened with the exertion of the climb and with the feeling of not being able to draw enough air into her lungs. She poked her head above the third-level platform with considerable relief. The first thing she saw was Josephine's back.

"I hope he didn't follow you," Josephine said, not turning.

"No, I'm alone." Martha stepped out onto the floor.

The tower had sixteen windows, two in each of the eight sides. All were intact; the broken one had been replaced. Martha remembered the pointed roof and the killer whale on the rod at the peak.

Josephine stood looking out at the water. Martha moved up beside her. "He's not down there listening?" Josephine spoke in a half whisper.

"No."

Window seats with red and pink velveteen pads circled the tower. Josephine sat down and looked at Martha. "I saw Diego," she said. "In town. He went by the store and didn't see me, and I didn't even think—I just ran to him."

"What happened?"

Josephine glanced down at her hands, then up through her lashes at Martha. "He said not to tell anyone. He said he'd get in touch. He said—wait." Josephine put her fingers on Martha's arm. "Please don't tell Jules. Or Dr. Marston."

"But why can't Diego come to the house and call on you like any friend of yours? Why must he . . .?"

Josephine gripped Martha's arm, her fingers digging in. "They wouldn't let him see me. They turned the girls I used to know away. I sat here in the tower and saw them leave. They don't want me to have daddy's money—they want me to die."

"Who?"

"Jules. Aunt Natalie."

A persecution complex, the doctor had said. Martha watched Josephine.

"Oh, you don't believe me, I can tell. You talked to Dr. Marston today, and he told you I really did try to kill myself. But I didn't. I don't want to die."

"Maybe with the drugs you were taking, you. . . ."

"I don't take drugs anymore. Dr. Marston got me to stop, and when I did I could think better. And I knew I didn't dare take barbs again because someone was after me. I didn't dream I was pushed off the cliff—I really was. Oh, I know he told you about the times I overdosed. Only I didn't. Someone gave me the pills. In something I ate or drank. I'm careful now. Please believe me, Martha. I know you can't be a spy for Aunt Natalie, because she's angry about you being here. And I can tell you don't know

Jules very well—besides, he watches you. So I think I can trust you. There's no one else to trust except Sarah, and she's just a little girl.''

"I won't mention Diego unless I think he's going to cause trouble,'' Martha told her. ''But you're sure it was Diego?''

"He looks older—but I'd know him anywhere. Oh, Martha. . . .'' Josephine smiled slowly, her face radiant.

Martha, seeing the vulnerability in her face, thought of Josephine's immaturity. *I'll keep her safe,* she vowed. *This Diego, whoever he is, will answer to me.* "I want to meet Diego,'' Martha said.

"All right,'' Josephine answered dreamily. ''You'll see how wonderful he is. And you can help us. . . . Before, I thought I had to live without Diego, and I was trying. If I hadn't lost those two years, maybe it wouldn't have been so hard, I would have had two more years of trying. I was even beginning to forget a little and see that other men were attractive.''

What other men? Martha wondered. When did Josephine see any other men except the ones in the house?

"I dreamed about Cathleen last night,'' Josephine said. ''When Cathleen's here, there're parties and people come to Black Tor and everyone laughs more. Even Jules.''

Cathleen? Another cousin. Wasn't she—Charn's sister?

"Only my dream was strange,'' Josephine went on. ''There was a fire and a man dressed in a black robe, and you were there. . . .'' Josephine shook her head. ''I didn't like the dream. Why couldn't I have dreamed of Diego, instead?''

"You'll let me know when you hear from him again?'' Martha asked.

"Yes.''

"Shall we go downstairs now?''

"Don't you like the tower, Martha?''

Martha stood and looked out the windows, turning slowly. She could see men working among the shrubbery and Henry polishing the Rolls near an outbuilding she thought must be the garage. Boats dotted the blue water, and she could see the mountains on the mainland. "The view is spectacular," she said.

"I see everything," Josephine told her. "No one knows how much I see from the tower." She stood beside Martha.

An open-topped red sports car rushed up the drive and stopped in front of the house.

"Oh—that's Cathleen!" Josephine cried. "I should have known she was coming when I dreamed of her last night." She started down the spiral staircase. "You must meet Cathleen."

The words floated back up to Martha as she watched a blond woman alight from the car. She'd thought of Cathleen as dark. But, of course, Charn was fair.

Had he been the one in her room last night?

Martha came down from the tower to meet Cathleen. Josephine waited impatiently for her in the hall, and they found Cathleen in the library, perched on the edge of Jules's desk, chattering gaily. She turned when they came into the room.

Her hair was golden-blond and curled under gently where it touched her shoulders. Her eyes were a pale blue-green, matching a pastel knit pantsuit that clung to her, revealing an excellent figure.

"Well, Josephine," she said, "I've brought you a painting, the one I've promised for so long—I do keep my promises sooner or later." The pale eyes flicked to Martha and her eyebrows raised. "The new nurse?" She turned back to Jules. "Has Natalie softened up? I thought she mistrusted anyone under fifty."

"I hired Miss Jamison." Jules said.

"Oh?"

A small word, and yet Cathleen managed to insinuate—what? That she knew very well the reason Jules had hired Martha?

Martha found herself bristling with dislike as the blond head turned back to her. "I'm Martha Jamison," she said, forcing calmness into her tone.

Two small creases appeared between Cathleen's brows. "You're from the States. Seattle?"

"No—that is, only very recently."

"I thought perhaps I'd seen you there. But...." Cathleen allowed the words to trail off.

Martha tensed. *She's going to recognize me from those horrid pictures in the papers,* she thought.

Cathleen shook her head and turned away. "I've asked a few people over for the weekend," she said to Jules. "All right?"

"If you've invited them already, what else can I say?" he asked dryly.

"Are you going to have a party?" Josephine wanted to know.

"If you'd like one." Cathleen smiled.

"Back, I see." Charn's voice startled Martha. Once again he'd come up so quietly she hadn't heard him.

"Hello, dear brother Charn." Cathleen's voice held nothing of affection but seemed to mock.

"Just can't stay away, can you?" he said.

"At least I manage to leave once in a while."

Jules stood up and instantly Cathleen turned back to him. "We'll have a party, then, Jules, shall we? For Josephine."

"And Martha, too," Josephine said, linking her arm in Martha's. "You'll come to the party, won't you?"

"Of course she will," Cathleen said.

Martha had a moment's panic, thinking of meeting a

group of strangers. Could she count on no one associating her with Marty Collier? Then she remembered that someone at Black Tor already knew but preferred to keep his knowledge a secret. Her eyes flicked from Charn to Jules, but they were both watching Cathleen.

"I'll tell Aunt Natalie," Jules said. "She likes to plan ahead. What night will the party be?"

"Saturday, of course." Cathleen held her hands out to Jules, and he took them in his. "Oh, it's good to be home," she said, looking at him.

Martha thought the two of them might have been alone. She pushed away the prick of jealousy. What reason did she have to resent Jules's attraction for his cousin? And Cathleen *was* pretty.

Martha turned away and met Charn's knowing smile. She tried to slip quietly out the door, but then she encountered Natalie in the foyer.

"Oh, there you are, Miss Jamison. My brother would like to meet you. I'll ask you to remember he's a sick man and to keep the visit short." Natalie's tone was brisk but neutral.

Martha followed the older woman up the stairs. Then she turned to the left, away from the corridor that led to Martha's room, and walked to the end of a similar hall. Natalie opened a door, and they came into a sitting room full of heavy mahogany furniture, the pieces so crowded together that Martha felt stifled. A large black dog stood stiffly by the door as though guarding the room against strangers, but Martha no more than glanced at it. She knew by then there were no live animals at Black Tor.

Natalie led her through this room and into a bedroom beyond, where a hospital bed dominated the scene. An oxygen tank stood tall and green beside the bed. A man rose from a chair as they entered, and Martha recognized the muscular young man she'd caught a glimpse of from the parlor.

"We won't need you for a few minutes, Simon," Natalie said.

The man came around the bed toward them. He kept looking at Martha.

Martha shifted her eyes. Should she introduce herself, since Natalie had neglected to do so? She hesitated, then drew back as Simon brushed against her in passing. Surely that hadn't been necessary. She watched him go out the door.

"Simon looks after my brother," Natalie said.

"Is that you, Nat?" A man's voice, thin but clear, came from the bed.

Martha turned toward him and stopped in surprise.

Natalie paid her no attention. "I didn't realize you were awake, Norman. Shall I raise the bed?"

"I'd like my head up a little more, yes."

Natalie pushed a button, and the head of the bed rose so that Norman Garrard was in a sitting position.

Now Martha saw that he was not an exact duplicate of the portrait of his father that hung in the dining room. His face was thin to the point of emaciation, and his beard and hair were shot with gray, lessening the impact of the white streaks.

"This is Martha Jamison, who's come to be with Josephine. You wanted to meet her."

"Come over here, Martha. Let me look at you."

Martha approached the bed.

"A pretty young woman. Always like a pretty nurse, myself. I suppose that's why you found Simon for me, Nat. You never were one to let a person indulge his whims."

His color was poor, bluish around the lips. *Heart,* Martha thought.

"I'll want her to read the family history. Don't argue with me about it, Nat. Just be good enough to get the book—it's in the bookcase in the other room."

Natalie pursed her lips and went out the door.

Norman Garrard leaned toward Martha. "Watch Josephine," he whispered. "Don't let them take her away."

"I'm here to care for her." Martha, too, spoke softly.

"You don't understand. She's never been mad—they just want you to think so. Last year—" He stopped speaking, and she saw that his eyes were fixed on the door where Natalie was reentering the room.

CHAPTER EIGHT

"I BELIEVE YOU'VE EXCITED YOURSELF, Norman," Natalie said as she came toward the bed, carrying a calf-bound book. "We'll run along—you must rest."

Martha saw that he'd closed his eyes. Without the intent gaze of his brown eyes, he looked dead. She resisted the inclination to feel his pulse, which she knew would be weak and thready. Chronic congestive heart disease, she decided. "Goodbye, Mr. Garrard," she said softly. "I'm glad we've met."

"Talking tires him," Natalie offered. "He's eighty-five, after all, and he should know better than to exert himself. What did you say to him?"

"Nothing of any importance. He wondered how I liked my job."

At the head of the stairs, Natalie held out the book. "He insisted on you reading this. Frankly, I don't think you'll be interested. I didn't want to argue with him and upset him. Of course, you don't have to take the book at all. As long as he thinks—"

"I'd like to read the Garrard family history," Martha cut in. "I know so little of this area." She took the book from Natalie. "Thank you."

Natalie shrugged and went down the stairs.

Martha hesitated, then decided to put the book in her room before finding Josephine.

But Josephine was waiting in Martha's room. Her eyes glistened with excitement. "Oh, everything's so much better since you came!'' Josephine exclaimed. "You're lucky. I knew you were when I touched the coral necklace. And now Cathleen's home and there'll be a party!''

"Your cousin's very pretty,'' Martha said.

"Oh—Cathleen? Yes. Men like her.'' Josephine giggled. "Only Jules holds out—she can't get Jules.''

"I thought he seemed quite. . .interested.''

"Maybe. But he's never going to get married again. That's what Cathleen wants. Because of the money.''

"I thought you liked Cathleen.''

"I do. She's fun. But the money's mine. And Jules's, too. When daddy dies.'' She got up from the chair by the window and came toward Martha. "You saw him just now, didn't you? He's going to die soon, isn't he?''

Martha turned away, her skin prickling uneasily. Norman Garrard had said his daughter wasn't mad. Perhaps not, but could this be called normal, this—this ghoulish waiting for death?

"He has a serious heart condition,'' she said.

"That man came,'' Josephine said.

"What man?'' This jumping from topic to topic could merely be restlessness, but many patients at Camarillo had done the same, flitting from one subject to another, like hummingbirds at a blossoming shrub.

"Why, the man who knows you, the one you met on the boat.'' Josephine's eyes glinted with mischief.

Where had she heard about that. . .? Still, Martha had been warned that Josephine listened at doors. "If you mean Branwell Lowrey,'' Martha told her, "he has business with your brother.''

"I know. What's he look like? Is he short and red-haired like the Bronte Branwell? I never heard of anyone else being named that.''

Martha shook her head. "He has brownish hair—and a

beard. I can't remember if Branwell Bronte sported a beard."

Josephine was silent for a moment. "I didn't get to see him, but I'll watch when he leaves," she said at last.

"Do you like to read?" Martha asked, wanting to change the subject. "You mentioned the Brontes...."

"Yes. I've read everything about them—the girls mostly, not their beastly little brother. I hated him. He couldn't even paint, much less write, but the fuss was always about him and not Charlotte or Emily. Imagine being able to write something like *Wuthering Heights*."

"Catherine's love was an obsession," Martha said.

"But isn't love always if you can't have the man you want?" Josephine asked. "And for the man, too—Heathcliff was equally obsessed."

"He was strange from the beginning," Martha argued, "while Catherine could have led a normal enough life if she hadn't encountered him. I've always felt so."

"Like me?" Josephine said. "Would I have been 'normal' if I hadn't met Diego?"

"You're not—abnormal," Martha said.

"Yes, I am, and you know it. But I'm not crazy." She came close to Martha. "Let's go on a picnic tomorrow. I haven't been on a picnic since—for a long time. We can ask Sarah. She says I never do anything with her, so she can come, too."

Martha hesitated, remembering what Jules had said.

"Oh, we won't go off the grounds—I know Jules won't let us. But there're nice places here, places where we can be alone."

"All right. I haven't been on a picnic since I was a little girl," Martha said.

"I'll tell Elsa to fix us a basket with hot chocolate to drink. Do you want to choose the food or be surprised?" Josephine asked.

"I'd prefer coffee, sugar only," Martha told her. "Otherwise I like surprises."

Josephine narrowed her eyes. "I don't think you do, not really. You're a Capricorn, and they always like to know exactly where they are."

"How did you know I was a Capricorn?"

"You act like one. I can usually tell. Cathleen's a Gemini—very charming. Of course, you can't trust her. But, then, I don't trust people much, anyway. And Sarah's a Sagittarius, arrow straight."

"What are you?" Martha asked.

"A Scorpio. That's why I have secret knowledge of things. Scorpios do."

"Then your birthday is soon."

"Oh, yes. Soon. And daddy promised me he wouldn't change his will like Jules wants. So I'll have money, and then I'll leave. Diego will come and get me, he'll take me away from Black Tor and I'll be safe forever."

"Does—does Diego know about the money?"

Josephine shook her head and laughed. "I know what you're thinking. But he doesn't know—how could he? It's me—he loves me, and he's come back for me."

Then why doesn't he come to the house? Martha thought. *Why doesn't he meet your brother and ask to see you here?* But she remained silent.

"Daddy gave you the history—are you really going to read it?" Josephine pointed to the book Martha still held.

"Yes."

"There've been others like me—you'll find out. That's when I knew I wasn't mad at all—when daddy gave me the book to read." Josephine sat on the bed.

"You expect me to be sorry about him dying, don't you? But it was too late when he started paying attention to me. I couldn't pretend to love him. He never loved me or my mother. Only Jules's mother. He even named me after her.

His Josie. That's why I won't let anyone use a nickname for me. No one called *her* Josephine, even if it was her real name. She was always Josie.''

Josephine got up with a sudden movement and brushed past Martha. "I'm going to my room. I'll leave the door open, though, so you can come in if you want later on.''

After Josephine went out, Martha lay on the bed and began thinking of Simon, the man who took care of Norman Garrard. Could Simon have been the one in her room the night before? She hadn't liked the way he'd looked at her—not at all....

She picked up the history of the Garrard family.

"If Abel Garrard had been in the right place at the right time, he would have, without question, become a pirate and a very capable one,'' the book began. Martha read of how he'd made a fortune in sealing and built Black Tor in 1880, when he tired of rented quarters. Norman, his first child, was born ten years later. Old Abel had turned up his nose at building on the fashionable streets in Victoria. Not for him a mansion along Rockland Avenue next to Robert Irving's or Rout Harvey's. He wouldn't have a Stoney-hurst, but he'd have Black Tor, built where he wanted his home. Apart from others as he felt himself apart from the common run of humanity. The prominent of Victoria be damned.

With mounting horror, Martha read of the cruelties of the sealing industry. When so many of the breeding females had been killed off that the seal population declined, Abel Garrard, foreseeing the death of the industry, sold his boats and got out before the market plummeted. He then managed to latch on to the very profitable market for outfitting eager gold seekers on their way to the Klondike. He made still more money. Victoria boomed with the Canadian-Alaskan gold rush.

Norman's mother had died only a few years after his

birth, and Abel raised the boy as best he could with a succession of Indian and Scottish housekeepers. He didn't marry for years. Then, when Norman was eighteen, Abel surprised everyone by his marriage to a young woman. This second wife in due time produced Natalie, but then she succumbed to "galloping consumption." So much death among the Garrard women....

So Norman had been raised without a mother—as Josephine had been, Martha thought sleepily. And how about Sarah? What had become of her mother, whoever she was? Had Jules bought her off, or was she dead, too?

Martha jerked herself awake. *I shouldn't sleep,* she thought. Rising, she made her way to Josephine's room.

Josephine was lying face down on the bed. She sat up and glared at Martha. "What are you doing in here?"

Martha stepped backward. "I thought you didn't mind if I came in."

Josephine's eyes were redrimmed, as though she'd been crying. "Why can't you leave me alone? I don't care what Dr. Marston told you—I won't try to kill myself. Stop watching me!"

"I'll be next door if you want me," Martha told her as she left.

What was wrong with Josephine now?

After an uneventful dinner, Martha returned to her room and locked the door. Then, recalling Dr. Marston's words, she turned off her light, lifted the lithograph from the wall and peered into Josephine's room. *It's no worse than looking through the window slit at a psychotic patient behind the locked doors at Camarillo,* she told herself. Still, Josephine wasn't psychotic. Or was she? Martha shifted from one foot to the other as she watched Josephine, then turned away as the girl began to undress. *I don't like spying,* Martha thought, and got into her bed.

The next she knew, the room was bright with morning.

Her eyes flew to the clock beside her bed. Eight! She hurried to the peephole and saw that Josephine's bed was empty, but she could hear water running and thought the girl might be taking a shower. Martha hung the lithograph back in place and hurried to dress herself. She wore khaki denim pants with a rust-colored buttoned shirt that she left open at the neck. Would Josephine still plan on the picnic, or would she have a new whim that day?

She unlocked her door and knocked at Josephine's.

Josephine's eyes were clear when she came out of her room—no sign of the previous day's tears. "You haven't forgotten about the picnic?" she asked.

"No, I dressed purposely for it."

"We can leave about ten-thirty—Sarah will be through with her morning lessons by then."

Lessons? Oh, yes, with Louella Gallion, the cousin who had retired from schoolteaching. Louella, who never spoke at the table.

"Where are we going?" Martha asked.

Josephine glanced at her sideways. "You said you liked surprises."

Martha frowned at something odd in Josephine's voice. She looked at her, but Josephine's face was averted.

They ate breakfast with Cathleen.

"A wonderful day for painting," Cathleen said. "Look at that sky. I'm going down to the cove and paint corny water scenes until I drop."

"What do you do in Seattle?" Martha asked. "Do you have a gallery?"

"I should be so fortunate." Cathleen's voice was rueful. "No, I'm in commercial art. Tiresome, but a living."

"Where's my picture?" Josephine asked.

"Oh, it's still in the car—I forgot to bring it in last night. Hold on—I'll get it now." Cathleen put down her coffee cup and went out.

The canvas was large—at least three feet by four.

"You got it right," Josephine said, her eyes shining. "How did you know, Cathleen?"

"A fishing boat you asked for, a fishing boat you got," Cathleen answered. She smiled, seemingly gratified by Josephine's pleasure.

"Look, Martha, see how the nets go up here like this? Have you ever seen a salmon boat?"

"Not that I paid attention to," Martha replied.

She gazed at the painting. The boat stood by a wooden dock at sunset. The fishermen were gone, only a few gulls remained, not flying but perched on the posts of the pier. Like mourners, Martha thought unexpectedly. The work was skillfully done, but the picture depressed Martha. Was it the color? Red with the sun setting? No, not exactly, though the red was disquieting—a bloody red. *I don't like it,* she thought. *I feel as though everyone isn't just home having supper but permanently gone. Dead. The boat will rot and the gulls fly away.* She shivered involuntarily and tried to mask it by rising and pouring herself more coffee.

At ten-thirty Sarah skipped into the foyer, where Martha and Josephine waited for her, and the three of them went out into the woods. Martha wondered where they were in relation to what she'd seen from the tower windows. She turned around and tried to tell. Although she could see the tower rising white, the windows glittering in the sun, there were too many trees between them and the house to pinpoint their position.

"I could easily get lost," Martha said.

"No, you couldn't," Sarah told her. "You can always see the tower, so you don't have to worry."

They came out at last onto a promontory where rock pushed through the ground. Geraniums grew in the soil between the rocky outcrops and tumbled in colorful fountains over the cliff edge. Sarah ran and peered over, while Martha caught her breath in alarm.

"Sarah—be careful!" she called after her.

"Oh, I won't fall. I'm a—I'm an ibex. That's a mountain goat." She grinned widely, then scampered back the way they'd come. "I saw some blackberries," she said. "I'm going to pick them."

Josephine dropped the blanket she'd been carrying, then bent to spread it out, and Martha set down the basket.

"We're not—are we going to eat right on the cliff?" Martha asked.

"Why not? There's a wonderful view. Look." Josephine threw out her hand in a gesture that took in the water, the sky, the islands and the mainland of Canada and the United States.

Martha wondered at her own uneasiness. Heights had never bothered her. She approached the verge and looked down. High enough that a fall might well be fatal—especially with the boulders at the bottom. If not, one could drown in the water lapping at the base. She glanced back and was disconcerted to find Josephine directly behind her, her hands half raised.

"Were you thinking of how lucky I was?" Josephine asked. "I haven't been back here since the day someone pushed me over."

CHAPTER NINE

MARTHA LOOKED BEHIND JOSEPHINE, but Sarah was no-where in sight. A tingle of fear ran along her spine.

"Of course *I* wouldn't push *you* over," Josephine said.

Was there a touch of mockery in her voice? Martha took a step toward her, and Josephine turned aside to let her pass. Surely she'd imagined the implied threat. Why would Josephine wish to harm her?

"The insane have their own logic." Who'd told her that? One of the doctors at Camarillo, most likely. "Don't think they can't reason—it's only that they reason from their own reality, instead of the one we recognize."

Was Josephine's reality so different that it didn't fit into the real world?

Despite the sun glittering on the water and warm on her shoulders, Martha felt cold. A fresh breeze blew across the promontory. An unlikely place to choose for a picnic. Why had Josephine brought her there?

"How—what were you doing when you fell?" Martha asked.

"I didn't fall. I'd been sitting on a blanket reading, and the next thing I knew I was home in bed."

"I found her." Sarah's voice startled Martha.

She turned and saw the girl standing beside her, mouth stained by blackberries.

"I was sort of following Jo—she used to yell at me when she caught me, but I did, anyway. Then she started to read, so I went to see if I could find any chestnuts, and I heard something—I don't know, a kind of noise like maybe Ahlmakoh would make—and I was a little scared so I ran out of the woods toward the cliff, but no one was here. Only the book and the blanket and the basket. At first I thought maybe he really had gotten Jo, and I wanted to run, but I looked over the edge in case...."

"There's a rock about ten feet down," Josephine said. "I'd gotten lodged there, somehow. I don't know how they ever got me back up."

"Bill Wong climbed down with a rope," Sarah said. "Henry helped him. It was real exciting."

"This is the first time I've been back," Josephine said.

"Who did you think you heard in the woods?" Martha asked Sarah.

"Oh, that's those Indian legends Matthew tells her," Josephine said. "Ahlmakoh is sort of a—a woods demon, I guess you might say."

"Do you believe he's real?" Martha asked Sarah.

"Not exactly," Sarah said. "Mostly I'm not afraid in the woods. But it was a *funny* noise."

Sarah walked over and opened the basket lid. The cook had fixed egg and salmon-salad sandwiches. There was a thermos of coffee, as well as one of hot chocolate, and apples, cheese and peanut butter cookies for dessert. The food was well prepared, and Martha enjoyed her salmon-salad sandwich, but she found the coffee so bitter it was almost undrinkable and swallowed only enough to wash down the bread and later a cookie.

"Do you want to pick blackberries?" Sarah asked. "I know where they are."

They were sitting on the blanket, and the breeze had lessened, making the spot more pleasant. Martha looked at the green islands against the blue water and thought she'd never seen anything quite so beautiful. The clear sharpness of the colors was different from the tropical lushness of the

Hawaiian Islands, although, come to think of it, she felt some of the same languor. . . .

"I'm going to read," Josephine said.

"I think I'll just sit here and relax," Martha told Sarah.

Martha watched Sarah walk away from the cliff, then stretched out alongside Josephine, who was lying on her stomach, the book open in front of her.

"I'm so sleepy," Martha complained. "I can hardly keep my eyes open."

She saw Josephine glance at her, and then that was all she remembered until she heard a child screaming somewhere.

Why couldn't she open her eyes? Martha wondered. That child, whoever it was, needed help. She was a nurse, she could help. . . . But the soft darkness held her suspended. Too much effort to wake up. Best to forget, to sleep. . . .

"Mar-tha!"

Her name, the girl was calling her name—shrieking, rather. Sarah? Was it Sarah?

Martha opened her eyes. All she could see was water, dark blue water swirling into white foam over the black rocks below her. She blinked, trying to clear her head.

"Martha! Please wake up and move—you're going to fall."

It *was* Sarah's voice. Martha tried to raise her head and realized with a sudden jolt of terror that she was lying on the very edge of the cliff. She scrabbled backward as best she could, sending a shower of dirt and broken geraniums down the cliffside.

"Oh, Martha, I thought you'd never hear me!" Sarah said.

Martha crawled away from the cliff, unable to trust herself to stand. She felt dizzy and uncoordinated. The blanket surely hadn't been that close when she'd gone to sleep. . . .

Sarah grasped the corner of the blanket and pulled it away from the cliff edge. "Why did you move the blanket over?" she asked Martha. "You almost fell like Jo."

Josephine! Where was she? Martha looked around, her head spinning. She caught her breath—had Josephine gone over the edge?

She stared at the little girl, with her blackberry-stained hands and mouth. Obviously Sarah had been in the woods again. "Did you see anyone?" she asked. "Where's Josephine?"

"Jo's gone somewhere. She was gone when I came back."

Involuntarily Martha stared at the cliff.

"Jo's not down there," Sarah said with an unbelievable calmness. "I looked. She must have gone for a walk."

Martha tried to organize her thoughts. First of all, she'd been drugged. It wasn't hard to connect that with the bitter coffee. Thank God she hadn't had much of it. Barbiturates? If so, the coffee must have been really supersaturated for her to be so affected from the small amount she'd drunk.

She remembered telling Josephine the day before that she'd rather have coffee than hot chocolate. Had Josephine drugged the coffee to get her out of the way for a while? Out of the way permanently? Why? Operating on her own logic?

"We've got to find Josephine," Martha said to Sarah. "Where do you think she went?"

Sarah shook her head and shrugged.

Martha got slowly to her feet, clutching at the girl's shoulder for support.

"Don't you feel good?" Sarah asked.

"I'll be all right." But she swayed, unable to walk. As her legs gave way under her, she saw a man come out of the woods. Jules. She was helpless, falling forward, the blackness closing in. . . .

Martha roused to voices: "Couldn't wake her up. I knew something was wrong so I . . . ."

Martha opened her eyes and saw Josephine's concerned face above hers. Jules was kneeling beside her. "How do you feel?" he asked.

"Groggy. The coffee . . . ."

"Oh, of course," Josephine said. "Sarah and I didn't drink any coffee."

"Can you walk if we help you?" Jules asked.

"I'll try," Martha said. "It should help clear my head. Exercise."

Jules assisted her to her feet.

"I had to pull the blanket back from the edge of the cliff," Sarah said. "It was right there." She pointed. "I made Martha wake up so she didn't fall."

Josephine clutched at Martha's arm, eyes wide with what looked like genuine panic. "Did you move that close to the edge, Martha?"

"I—I don't know what happened," Martha said.

When they got back to the house and up to her room, she fell asleep almost immediately, not rousing until she became aware of a persistent tapping.

The room was dark. Martha sat up in bed, the coverlet falling away from her. *I'm dressed,* she thought in confusion. *But it's night. . . .*

Someone was rapping at her door. She flicked on the bedside light and saw that it was nine o'clock. Her mouth tasted stale and her head throbbed. She made her way to the door and opened it.

Jules stood in the hall with a tray. "I watched Elsa fix this food," he said. "I can vouch for it."

If you *can be trusted,* Martha thought. She stood aside, and he entered the room. She tried to smooth her hair and was conscious of her rumpled clothes.

"I'm sorry to have to wake you, but we must talk," Jules said.

Martha excused herself and went to the bathroom, where she washed her face, donned a clean shirt and brushed her hair quickly.

When she reentered the bedroom, Jules had taken the cover from the tray, which he'd set on a small table. He pulled a second chair near the table. "I'll have tea with you, if you'll be so kind as to pour," he said.

She was glad it wasn't coffee.

"Elsa knows nothing about what was in the coffee," he said. "I tasted what was left in the thermos. Bitter as hell. I asked her what she'd done with the picnic basket when she had it filled. Apparently it sat on a table in the foyer until the three of you were ready." Jules watched her for a moment. "Eat your soup," he said. "If you want me to have some just in case...."

"No, I'm—sure the soup isn't drugged," Martha said, picking up a spoon. The soup was a delicious fish chowder and she ate it all.

"I imagine you won't be staying on," Jules said as she spooned up the last mouthful.

Martha glanced at him. She'd been too foggy to feel very frightened over what had happened to her. "Do you want me to leave?" she asked quietly.

"I don't want anything to happen to you. I may as well be honest with you now. Josephine's last nurse, Miss Eccles, had a bad fall here in the house. She tripped coming down the main staircase one night. She—refused to call it an accident."

Martha stared at him. His face was pale, and a muscle twitched in his jaw. Why was he so upset about the nurse?

"Is she—has she recovered?"

"She's still at St. Joseph's. It was a bad break—the

femur shattered and she needed surgery. We hope she'll be able to walk eventually.''

''Was she—pushed?'' Martha asked.

''I had myself convinced she was confused,'' Jules said. ''But now you....''

''I don't really remember much,'' Martha said. ''I was lying at the cliff edge when Sarah roused me enough that I could crawl back to safety. I don't know how I got there. The last I recall is watching Josephine pick up her book to read and feeling sleepy.''

''Josephine says she thought you were asleep at first, but when she couldn't wake you, she became frightened and ran to the house for help. Apparently Sarah had wandered off to pick berries?''

''Yes. Sarah wasn't there when I fell asleep.''

Jules shook his head. ''I didn't want to think Josephine had anything to do with Miss Eccles's accident. And I don't want to blame her now. But....''

''Why do you?''

He glanced at her sharply. ''She's not—normal. I've fought against the idea that she's deranged, but now I'm not so sure.''

''But why does it have to be Josephine who pushed the other nurse and drugged me?''

''The alternative is to imagine some outsider creeping around Black Tor—''

''With a grudge against nurses?'' she interrupted tartly.

''No one in the house could be responsible for such things,'' Jules said. ''All the servants except Simon have been with us for years. And he's with my father.''

''Josephine's been involved in three accidents herself,'' Martha reminded him. ''Have you ever once considered them as anything other than suicide attempts?''

Jules stared at her. ''Miss Eccles mentioned something similar,'' he said. ''She wondered about the last drug overdose, when Josephine broke a window. Miss Eccles wasn't sure Josephine had taken the drugs on purpose. But what else is possible? Dr. Marston thinks she changed her mind after she swallowed them.''

"Do you know where Josephine was those two years she was away from Black Tor?'' Martha asked. "I was amazed that any doctor would take on a case without full cooperation from the family.''

"It's not necessary to discuss that,'' Jules said. "I'd appreciate it if you'd stay on until we can make other arrangements for Josephine.'' He frowned. "Perhaps we shouldn't try to keep her at home any longer. She might be happier in....''

Martha clamped her lips together to prevent words of disagreement from pushing out. She must be careful with Jules. Was the money that Josephine could inherit any day now influencing him? Was he to blame, as Josephine thought?

"I'm not afraid to stay on here,'' she said. "Unless, of course, you prefer to dismiss me. I believe you accused me of being involved in some conspiracy to take your whale away. Perhaps you don't trust me.''

Jules waved his hand. "Oh, that. I'm sorry about flaring up. I talked to young Lowrey yesterday afternoon. He's on loan to our museum from the University of California at San Diego. He *is* interested in the whale, but only because of an article he's doing for a scientific journal on the orcas. I'm afraid I antagonized him with my suspicions. Seems a nice enough chap, but he didn't take to me at all.''

"Then you have no objection to me continuing to be Josephine's companion?'' Martha leaned forward and touched Jules's arm. "Please don't make any hasty decisions about your sister. She seems to trust me, and I'd like to try to help her.''

Jules stood up and drew her to her feet. "I don't want

you hurt,'' he said. Then suddenly he bent his head and kissed her, drawing her against him. His lips were not gentle. She responded with an intensity that shocked her.

Then he was gone.

Her mind began working again. Were those the arms that had held her down two nights earlier? Was Jules the man who knew she'd had a life other than the one as Martha Jamison? And why had she defended Josephine when it was quite likely the girl had drugged her so that she could run off and meet Diego without interference? The cliff edge...Martha shuddered with the memory of the dark water on the rocks below.

And now Jules telling her about Miss Eccles's accident.... Was she wrong about Josephine? Was Josephine dangerous?

CHAPTER TEN

JOSEPHINE AWAKENED HER EARLY, banging impatiently on her door. "I've eaten already," she told Martha. "And I'm going to be with Cathleen most of the day. She's fixing some surprise games for the party, and Sarah and I are going to help. You can, too, if you want."

Josephine's last sentence lacked enthusiasm, Martha thought. She dressed and went downstairs. Charn and Cathleen were at breakfast.

"You don't want to be mixed up in all the party doodads, Martha," Charn said. "I can tell you're not the type at all."

Was he mocking her?

"Besides, I've got all the help I need," Cathleen said.

Martha glanced from one to the other. Both blond, attractive—and up to something. What?

"Would you like to catch a salmon?" Charn asked. "Jules told me to get you away from the house today, to see that you have a rest."

Jules wants me to go? she wondered. *To leave Josephine with Cathleen? Maybe he no longer trusts me.*

Charn grinned. "I couldn't ask for a nicer assignment. If the fishing doesn't appeal to you, we could—"

"Oh, no. Salmon fishing is fine." Then she looked at him warily. Could Charn have crept into her room that first night? Did he know about her past?

He threw his arms up. "I'm harmless. Really, I am," he said.

"I'll be ready right after I eat," she said. "What should I wear?"

"Old jeans, old shoes and a warm jacket," Cathleen told her. "Josephine's got any number of old jeans if you didn't bring any. I have a jacket I paint in—quite beyond repair. You're welcome to it."

Martha accepted the jacket and went upstairs to borrow jeans from Josephine.

"Salmon fishing?" Josephine asked. "Do you really want to go?" She looked at Martha curiously.

"Do you mind?"

"Not with Cathleen here." Josephine's yellow eyes narrowed as she watched Martha's face. "Sometimes I wish you hadn't come at all."

"If not me, there would have been another nurse," Martha said.

"Oh, I know. But I might not have liked her—I'm used to that. I liked you, though, right away. I should have known better."

"Don't you like me now?" Martha stopped rummaging in her drawer. "Have I done something to make you unhappy?"

"*You* know," Josephine said.

Martha shook her head. "No. Tell me."

"What's the use?" Josephine's voice was sullen. "You're prettier than I am, and—and experienced and everything...."

"What on earth does that have to do with anything?" Martha asked in astonishment. "I think you're far prettier than I, whether you believe me or not. You're a striking young woman."

Josephine sat on Martha's bed. "There's something wrong with me!" she wailed. "There is, there is. And you...." She covered her face with her hands and began to cry. "I don't want you to stay here!" she sobbed.

"Just today or at all?" Martha asked.

"T-today." Josephine hesitated. "At least I know about you now. You might as well stay. But not today. Go away from me today. You make me feel bad."

Because you drugged me and pulled the blanket to the edge of the cliff? Martha wondered.

When Josephine had left the room, Martha changed into the borrowed jeans, which fit her a little too tightly, and a dark blue sweat shirt. Her tennis shoes were almost new, but they could be washed afterward, if need be. What was so dirty on a fishing boat?

"How old are you, anyway?" Charn said as they climbed into a yellow MG. "In that outfit you look like a teenager."

"I'm twenty-eight." She knew she looked younger with her hair down and a blue scraf tied to hold it back. But sometimes she felt a hundred years old. Surely Johann's last year should have etched a few permanent wrinkles on her face as it had on her mind. Johann, who had drugged her once, too, with a hallucinogen and then had laughed at her panic when she thought she was going mad. She'd never trusted him again.

"You haven't really fished for salmon until you've gone out in a dory," Charn said.

"You mean those big rowboats?" Martha asked. "I don't think I'd like to go out on the ocean in one of those."

"The ocean isn't on this side of the island." Charn was nearing a dock and he waved his hand. "To the left is the Strait of Georgia and to the right Juan de Fuca Strait."

"But the water's salty—it really is part of the Pacific Ocean," Martha argued.

"We don't think of it that way," Charn said. He stopped the MG and grabbed a jacket from the back.

Martha got out, with Cathleen's jacket over her shoulders. "Is this a private dock?" she asked.

"Ours. Well, Norman's, if you want to get technical. But he's generous enough with possessions. Jules, too, for that matter. Now money's different. . . ."

Martha stared at the tall-masted white boat beside the wooden piles.

"The boat's ours, too. Norman leases it out, though, so the captain can keep busy."

The Orca was painted on either side of the bow. The boat looked small compared to the ferry that had brought her to Vancouver Island, but at least it wasn't a dory.

"The gear is all aboard," Charn said. "Mike!" he called.

A dark-skinned man in a stocking cap came from the boat's small superstructure. "Hi, Charn," he said with easy familiarity.

"This is Martha Jamison," Charn told him. "A real beginner. Probably never saw a live salmon in her life." He turned to her. "Right?"

She nodded.

Mike grinned. "Glad to have you aboard, Martha," he said. "Beginners are lucky. We'll strike a real hog today, maybe."

"Weather going to hold all right?" Charn asked.

"Nothing snotty in sight," Mike confirmed. He raised his voice. "Get a hustle on, Vic. We're shoving off."

A teenage boy appeared from dockside and climbed aboard *The Orca*.

"The boat's named after the killer whale, isn't it?" Martha said to Charn as they eased out into the channel. "Are there any around here these days?"

"What do you mean 'these days'? This is killer-whale territory."

"I just wondered about them facing extinction like some of the other whales."

"Not the killer—they're too smart. Ever see one—a live one, I mean?"

"In a California Seaquarium once. Doing tricks."

"Come on." Charn pulled her along until they were standing by Mike. "Martha wants to see a killer whale. Think you can find a pod for her?"

Mike shrugged. "Maybe."

"A pod?" Martha asked.

"They travel in packs, like wolves," Mike said. "I used to ship out with an old Norwegian who called them 'fat choppers' because of the way they rush through a school of fish or seals and tear out hunks of meat, then come back and feed on the dying. As bad as sharks. Smarter, too."

"Do they attack people?" Martha asked.

"No," Charn said.

"Hell, yes!" Mike said. "They'll eat anything that's flesh and blood. Though I did hear one old Indian say they didn't like the taste of people and will spit them out."

"I never heard of anybody being attacked," Charn objected.

"Well, they don't come up underneath a swimmer and chomp off a leg like a shark," Mike agreed. "But there've been fishermen who didn't come back.... You still got that killer in the front hall at the house?"

Charn nodded.

"Give me the willies to live with it like you do." Then he turned to Martha. "We been catching mostly chinook. You hook into one of them, Martha, and you think you've lost him, but you haven't. He's just sulking around as far down as he can get. After a while he'll come to life. Seen it take two hours to land a big one."

"Don't salmon jump out of the water like other fish when they're caught?" Martha asked.

"Oh, a coho will. He's a showman. Gives you a hard fight, but a short one. We get mostly chinooks or kings right now. Some call them tyees, but that's local."

"You're not from around here?" Martha glanced discreetly at Mike's brown skin and black hair.

He grinned. "Came from Alaska before you made her a state. Like it better down here—hell of a lot warmer."

Martha watched the men check the bait on the trolling lines and took her place next to one of the poles, while Charn explained the mechanism. The water was a deep blue shading into brown. Gray-and-white gulls followed the boat.

Mike jerked his head at the birds. "They think we're going to hit lucky."

Charn got the first strike but swore as he yanked on the pole in reflex. "Damn it—I know better. Scared him off."

"Salmon's a nibbling fish," Mike explained to Martha. "Got to let them chew around awhile before you can set the hook."

Martha watched and waited, but nothing more happened, and she gradually turned away from the lines to look at the islands, dozens of them, all unbelievably green against the blue of sky and water. She leaned on the rail and breathed the cool wind. The sun touched her warmly and she felt at peace. Everything had been left behind at Black Tor. Josephine and her problems, even Martha's own past. There was only the sun and the water and. . . .

She jerked upright. A triangular fin, black, cut through the waves, paralleling the boat but going faster. And another. Three! She reached over and clutched at Charn's sleeve. "Sharks!" she cried, pointing at the fins.

Charn began to laugh. "Why, those are what you wanted to see, Martha. Those are the killer whales."

As he spoke, a black-and-white head broke through the water near the bow of the boat, hung there a second or two, then submerged. The fins moved off and soon were out of sight.

"No banquets here," Charn said.

"But he—it looked just like the one in California, like it was smiling. The one there lets her trainer put his head in her mouth."

"Geez!" Mike said. "You couldn't pay me enough to do a thing like that."

"Strike!" Vic yelled, and this time the chinook was hooked. Charn and Mike brought the salmon in after almost an hour of work.

After catching two smaller ones, Charn asked Martha if she wanted to go back, and she nodded. "I guess I'm a hypocrite," she said. "I like to eat salmon, but I hate to know they're on this boat with me, dying."

"Head her in!" Charn called to Mike.

"Come along again, Martha," Mike invited as she thanked him for the day. "We'll make you a real fisherman."

She climbed into the MG with Charn. "I'm glad you asked me to go," she said. "I do feel rested."

Charn had been different on the boat, she thought. Not so flip, not trying so hard to make an impression. She liked him better.

He caught her glance. "Will you come out with me again?" he asked. "Not on the boat, but maybe for lunch or dinner?"

She hesitated. "I don't know when I can get away."

"I'll fix it up with Jules ahead of time. Okay?"

"Well—yes, I'd like to."

He took her hand. "Jules should have thought of someone like you before. To hear Natalie, you'd think nurses *had* to be fat old cows." He smiled. "I could have been looking at you all this time, instead of that parade of crones."

Martha moved her hand, dislodging his.

"And Josephine likes you, too," he went on. "At least so far.... She seemed to get along with one or two of the others, but it never lasted. Not that I'm anyone to warn a psychiatric nurse—but don't forget that Josephine is...well, not normal. She can go along for a while and you think she ought to be out with others her age, having a good time—but then something happens to jolt you back to remembering she's got this mental aberration.'' Charn shook his head. ''The devil of it is—she's so pretty. Jules doesn't dare let her loose.''

A Volkswagen sat in the drive by the front of the house. Charn pulled past it and parked.

Martha thanked him again, then walked into the foyer, where the huge bulk of the killer whale shocked her anew as she thought of another black-and-white head peering at the boat earlier.

''Martha! I thought I was going to miss you again,'' a man's voice said.

She turned to see Bran Lowrey.

''Oh. Hello. I've just gotten back from salmon fishing.''

''So I heard. I came out today on the chance you'd be available to sightsee with me, but—''

''You know I have commitments,'' she said.

''Mr. Garrard was kind enough to talk to me again,'' Bran said. His voice held a note of—what? Distaste?

''Well, I'm sorry I wasn't here. Now I must—''

''He told me there was no reason you couldn't spend tomorrow afternoon in Victoria with me. So I'll come by about one-thirty, if that suits you.''

''Jules said—''

''He said you needed a few hours off. Please come with me.''

Why was she so reluctant to go? He really was a charming man. ''Thank you,'' she told him. ''One-thirty is fine.''

She walked up the steps to her room after Bran had left. Why was Jules so insistent on making her leave the house?

Josephine lay on Martha's bed, reading. "I thought you'd never get back," she said. "I wanted to tell you how wrong I was to think you were against me, too, like they are. I was right about you in the beginning—I can trust you." She stood up and hugged Martha. "You aren't mad at me, are you? You won't leave Black Tor?"

"I'm not going to leave," Martha said.

Josephine stepped back. "Oh, good," she said. "Because daddy's worse. Simon doesn't think he'll last the week. I'm going to need someone on my side."

CHAPTER ELEVEN

MARTHA HAD BREAKFAST the next morning with Josephine and Cathleen.

"I can hardly wait until tomorrow," Josephine said. "Aren't you excited, Martha?"

Martha nodded, but apparently the gesture wasn't convincing.

"Maybe she doesn't like parties," Cathleen said. "Or maybe we haven't invited the right man for her."

Martha sipped her coffee, not reacting to Cathleen. She hated being talked about as though she weren't present, as she was sure Cathleen was well aware.

"Oh, Martha will like *your* party, Cathleen." Josephine turned to Martha. "You will! We've worked out some surprises—wait until you find out what they are! People are coming from Seattle and Vancouver—and Cathleen's invited some of them to stay at Black Tor!" Josephine's eyes were shining with childlike enthusiasm.

Martha left the other two still talking at the table and went to find Jules. Halfway across the foyer, she heard someone call her name, and she glanced around, for a moment not recognizing the stocky figure on the staircase.

"Marty." Simon spoke in a husky whisper.

"My name is Martha," she said.

"Oh—sorry. Martha." He said her name deliberately, emphasizing the second syllable. "Mr. G. wants to see you. Right now."

"I'll just tell Jules where I'm going," Martha said.

"No!" Simon's voice rose as he glanced around uneasily. "Mr. G. wants it to be a secret."

"Why?"

Simon winked at her slyly. "How should I know? Never argue with money, is what I always say."

Martha hesitated, then started toward the staircase.

"How is Mr. Garrard?" she asked. "Josephine said he was—dying."

"That's been going on for months. But no denying he's worse." Simon nudged her arm familiarly. "Maybe the old man wants a last fling before he conks out."

Martha ignored the statement, but Simon wasn't easily discouraged.

"Maybe Mr. G. reads the same papers I do," he said.

Martha glanced at him.

He licked his lips. "I don't mind keeping it quiet," he said. "You could make it worth my while...."

"I don't know what you're talking about," she said, her heart sinking.

"Sure you do, Marty," he said. "Sure you do."

Simon knew. He'd been the one in her room.

"I don't care to continue this conversation with you, Simon." She strode past him and along the corridor, walking rapidly. She had almost reached Norman Garrard's suite when Simon caught up with her. He grasped her arm.

"Let me go," she said, her voice icy. "I won't be blackmailed. Take your hand off my arm or I'll scream. Then you can tell everyone who I am if you must, but I don't imagine you'll be kept on, either. Is that what you want?"

He scowled, dropping his hand. Martha walked through the door and into Norman Garrard's room. When she saw the old man propped against his pillows, she hurried to his bed, her fingers reaching automatically for a pulse. Congestive heart failure, certainly. He breathed in rapid shallow gasps.

Norman Garrard twitched his wrist away from her hand. A green nasal cannula was inserted in his nostrils to deliver oxygen from the tank beside the bed. Martha checked the gauge from habit. Despite the six liters of oxygen per minute, his lips were blue.

Martha turned her head and saw that Simon had come up next to her. "Has the doctor been here today?" she asked him.

"Don't need doctor." The old man spoke weakly, using as few words as possible, pausing between them. "No use. He knows. I know." His eyes flicked to Simon. "Outside," he said.

Simon left the room, shutting the door behind him.

"You. Only one can keep Josephine safe. Alive. Trust—you. Money. Too much. Greedy. Watch Josephine. Not crazy. Never was. I know. Only me. Sarah. Smart. Safe. Josephine—danger—you help. Too late. My fault."

"Is it the money Josephine will inherit when. . . ." Martha hesitated.

"When I die? Yes. Fair."

"And she's in danger because of this?"

"Yes."

"From whom?"

"Don't know. Them." His hands moved feebly. "One. More."

"In the house here, you mean?" Martha asked.

"Think so. Must be. I found Josephine. Brought her home. No sign of him. Dead."

"Him?"

"Young man. Two years."

Martha caught her breath. Josephine's father knew about Diego and the missing two years. But she couldn't tell him, a dying man, that Diego or someone pretending to be Diego was there in Victoria.

"I'll try to keep her safe," she told him.

"Stay alive as long as I can," he said. "Indian. I am. Garrards are. Part. Kwakiutl. Don't have word for sick man. Indians don't. Either live or die. Josephine must live. She's had—bad time. Tell her—"

The door flew open and Natalie marched into the bedroom. "What are you doing here?" she demanded, glaring at Martha.

"Sent for her," Mr. Garrard said.

"You should have known better than to come up here and bother him," Natalie said. "You, of all people—a nurse."

"Wanted her here," the old man repeated.

"Yes, and look how upset you are," Natalie scolded. "I'll have Simon give you something so you can rest. You know you're not up to talking."

He fixed his eyes on Martha's as she moved away from his bed. "Remember," he said.

Martha left the room, meeting Simon at the door. He glanced sideways at her as she passed, but he said nothing. Did he find Natalie and tell her she was there? Martha wondered. Or had she come by chance?

When she got downstairs, she found Jules in the library. "Am I disturbing you?" she asked.

He looked up from his desk. "No. Come in."

"I wanted to thank you for the salmon-fishing trip—I enjoyed every minute of the day."

"That was Charn's doing," Jules said. "He shamed me into it by calling attention to how pale you were after the—episode on the cliff. A day in the fresh air has brought back your color."

"Thank you. But I don't need another outing so soon after—"

"Nonsense. Let young Lowrey show you a bit of Victoria's beauty. Josephine is so engrossed in this coming party she won't even know whether you're here. Afterward...." He paused and his smile faded. "After her ups, her downs are bad," he said. "A complete mood change. You'll have to watch her carefully then. I wasn't too keen on Cathleen's party for that reason. But I can't keep Josephine shut away here with no entertainment." He looked down at the desktop, then back up at her. "Take the afternoon while you can," he said. "I only wish I...." He didn't finish the sentence.

"I just talked to your father," Martha said. "Natalie was quite angry with me. But he asked to see me."

Jules straightened in his chair. "Oh? What about?"

"He's worried about Josephine and wanted me to watch out for her."

"That's all?"

She nodded. "He's gravely ill," she said.

"Yes." Jules ran his hand over his face. "Yes," he repeated.

When he said nothing more, Martha left the library.

After lunch, Matthew Drew caught up with Martha before she reached the stairs on the way to her room. "Have you a few minutes?" he asked.

"Yes."

"We'll go into the music room—it's never used."

She followed him along a short corridor to the right of the foyer and through sliding doors, which he shut behind them. The room was blue and gilt, and there was a massive gold harp in the far corner. A stuffed Pekingese curled asleep at its base.

"Try not to upset Natalie," Matthew said as she faced him. His light eyes were watchful behind gray-rimmed glasses.

"She misunderstood," Martha began.

"Natalie does that," Matthew agreed. "But you must humor her. She isn't well, and I worry."

"I'll try to be careful," Martha said.

"Perhaps you'd be good enough to keep an eye on her while I'm gone. Since you're a nurse, you'd know if the doctor should see her."

"I've been hired to be with Josephine," Martha reminded him. "Of course, if I notice your wife looks ill, I'll certainly report that to Jules. But I can't promise to watch over Mrs. Drew."

"Just as long as you're aware," Matthew said. "I must get away soon. My research...." He paused, then added, "But I'm keeping you from something else."

"What research?" Martha asked politely, reluctant to hurt his feelings. He was younger than his wife—perhaps not even sixty yet, and not unattractive with his white hair and ruddy skin.

"Mysticism among the Vancouver Island Indians. A fascinating subject. The myths alone are a gold mine."

"Oh, yes," Martha said. "Sarah told me about Ahlmakoh. Do you tell her many of the—stories about demons? Because she's just a child and could be frightened by—"

"Are you criticizing my judgment?" Matthew demanded.

"Why, no. That is, I thought...."

"As you reminded me a few minutes ago, you were hired to care for Josephine, not to be Sarah's nursemaid." He glared at her.

"I'm sorry if I upset you," Martha said. "Please excuse me now—I have an appointment."

Martha hurried away from the music room and up the steps to her room. She put on the delft-blue pantsuit she'd worn when she'd met Bran on the ferry. Then she gathered up her purse and went down to meet him.

"You're looking well," he told her as he started the VW and swung around the drive. "No one would know you almost fell off a cliff the day before yesterday."

She stared. "How did you hear about that?"

"Let's say—an impeccable source."

Had Jules told him? Or had he been gossiping with the servants?

"I'm fine," she said shortly. "Where are we headed?"

"Would you believe Ye Olde English Tallyho?"

"What's that?"

"A tallyho is a sightseeing tour vehicle, I've been informed. In this case, horse drawn."

"That sounds like fun."

"Do you think I'd bore you?"

"Nothing about Victoria bores me," she said.

They got on the tallyho across from the museum. Martha remembered Jules pointing out the museum to her and asked Bran if he worked there.

"That's home base while I'm on the island," he said. "A fantastic layout they've got. You must see it before you leave."

She looked at him in surprise. "Before I leave?"

"Oh—just a manner of speaking. After all, Victoria isn't your home."

A few tourists boarded the tallyho, and then they were off on their sightseeing tour. Cy, the driver, kept up a steady stream of chatter, pointing out the local spots of interest and giving some details of the history of the island. After showing them the legislative buildings and the twenty-three-carat-gold statue of George Vancouver, they went on to Beacon Hill Park, given to the people of Victoria in 1858 by Sir James Douglas, the first governor of British Columbia, and from there to Goodacre Lake. Next, Cy pointed out Craigdarroch Castle, perched on its hill. Then they turned and drove along Park Boulevard. They passed the house were Emily Carr was born and grew up, then passed the totem poles in Thunderbird Park. When they came into the downtown section, Cy showed them the Christ Church Cathedral at the end of Courtney Street, pointing out the mandala in the upper window and the old burying ground next to the church.

Then finally they returned to the starting point.

"What a beautiful city!" Martha said to Bran after they'd climbed down onto the sidewalk. "Is it all so lovely?"

"Oh, there are meaner sections of town, but Victoria has nothing as bad as most American cities. Tourism is big business here. Quite a lot of money around."

"I didn't see many large homes."

"They're mostly in Oak Bay, except for some of the old ones like the castle the guide pointed out. And Black Tor, of course. I understand the Garrards were always—different." Bran's voice was hard.

"Did you quarrel with Jules?" Martha asked.

"Let's just call it mutual distaste."

Martha raised her eyebrows.

"Doesn't all his handsome perfection strike you as too good to be true?"

"I—I'd rather not discuss my employer, if you don't mind. Thanks for taking me out this afternoon. I did enjoy seeing more of the city."

"We'll take in something else next time. There's the Butchart Gardens and—"

"I may not have any time in the next week or so."

"Well, why not bring the girl along—what's her name? Josephine?"

"Oh, I don't think—"

"Why not? I'd rather see you with her along than not at all. She isn't really crazy, from what I understand."

"I hardly think it would be appropriate."

"Josephine probably would enjoy it, and her brother wouldn't refuse you, would he? I'd do my best to entertain Josephine so she wouldn't feel left out. I understand she's been shut up in that house for years. Poor kid.'' Bran shook his head.

Martha, watching him, thought perhaps he'd be good for Josephine. Cheerful, good-looking and not a native Victorian to be prejudiced about her. Bran might make her laugh and give her a few happy hours away from Black Tor. And there'd be two of them to keep track of Josephine—herself and Bran. If Josephine became depressed as Jules suggested she would after the party, Bran's idea might be a good one.

''I—I'll keep your invitation in mind,'' she told him.

CHAPTER TWELVE

BRAN DROVE MARTHA back to the house. As they turned into the drive, she saw Cathleen's red car ahead of them; when they pulled up before the house, Cathleen was just getting out. She walked over to Bran's VW.

"Hi. Enjoy your sightseeing?" Cathleen asked.

Martha nodded. "This is Bran Lowrey," she said. "Cathleen Wexler."

Cathleen smiled up at Bran. "No wonder Martha wasn't interested in my party," she said. "Now I understand. But I can remedy that. Bran, consider yourself invited. Informal. Tomorrow about six."

Bran sketched a bow. "Delighted," he said. "To meet you and to be invited to your party." He turned to Martha. "I'll see you tomorrow, then."

"A long-time friend?" Cathleen asked after Bran had driven away.

"No—I met him on the ferry coming over to Victoria."

Cathleen raised her eyebrows and smiled. "He's good-looking, if you like the candid blue-eyed type, and don't we all once in a while." She sighed. "Less trouble in the long run. At least you know where you stand."

Martha said nothing, but in her mind was Johann's handsome face, the clear, seemingly guileless eyes that had hidden his mind's dark thoughts. Bran wasn't Johann, of course, and she had no reason to suspect he was anything other than what he seemed. Still—Cathleen's generalization of candid-eyed types was seriously amiss. Who was

Cathleen thinking of? What man didn't let her know where she stood? Jules?

Had Jules held Cathleen and kissed her as he had kissed Martha? There was certainly no openness in Jules's glance, the deep brown eyes offered no easy interpretation of his thoughts. Again Martha relived the moments of terror of her first night at Black Tor. Could she be positive that the man had been Simon? If he had identified her, perhaps others had....

Cathleen walked away from her to the front door and Martha followed. Time to check on Josephine. Belatedly she realized that the girl was supposed to be spending the day helping Cathleen.

Once inside, Martha hurried upstairs, only to find Josephine reading quietly in her room. "Did you have fun?" she asked Martha.

"We took the tallyho tour," Martha said. "Victoria's the prettiest city I've ever seen. Each yard has flowers, and the houses are so neat and tidy."

"Not Black Tor," Josephine told her. "Daddy always said no architect could make the house fit in. He said it was a monstrosity and he was proud of it."

Martha sat on Josephine's bed. "Who brought you back here?" she asked. "Who found you in your lost years?"

"Why, daddy, of course—didn't I tell you?" Josephine said. "As soon as I saw him I knew who he was and who *I* was, too. That was in the States, somewhere. Daddy said Oregon."

"Where were you when he found you?"

"On a sort of farm with some other people. They were all older. When I remembered I was Josephine Garrard, I forgot who they were. Daddy told me their names but I still didn't know them."

"I had the impression that Jules was the one who brought you back," Martha said.

"Oh, no. I've heard him ask daddy about me, but daddy said it was none of his business. You're the only one I've told anything to."

"Then no one knows about your lost years except your father?"

Josephine frowned. "I don't know if he does, either. He told me he found me, but he won't talk about how I'd gotten where I was. And the people on the farm said they didn't know anything except that I'd been there a year and that someone had dropped me off with them."

"So you really have only one year accounted for?"

"I guess so. But I don't actually remember the farm, either. Only about the zodiac and my—occult learning. That came from the two years."

"Did your father ever mention how he located the farm?"

Josephine shook her head. "He wouldn't tell me."

Martha made up her mind to visit Norman Garrard again. He had wanted to tell her more before Natalie had interrupted. Was it about the missing years in Josephine's life? If he really believed his daughter was in danger, couldn't it be because of those two years? After all, she had always been his heir, hadn't she? She and Jules. Back to Jules again.

Martha rose from the bed. "Cathleen's invited Bran Lowrey to the party tomorrow," Martha said. "You'll have a chance to meet him. I think you'll like him."

Josephine clasped her hands together convulsively, dropping her book. "Maybe I will," she said after a moment. "Do you like him?"

"Yes," Martha answered.

"Do you think he's good-looking?"

"I suppose so, yes. Cathleen certainly thought so."

"Are you—interested in him?"

Martha glanced at Josephine, who smiled disarmingly.

"I don't know exactly how to put it. I like Bran, just as I like Charn. But—interested...?"

Josephine looked at her slyly under her lashes. "You like Jules better, don't you? Cathleen does and you do, too. I can tell. Well, you'd best be careful. Jules can be ruthless. Cynthia was terrified of him before she—died."

"In an accident?" Martha said.

Josephine laughed shrilly. "Yes, an accident. She fell down the stairs and broke her neck. Like I was supposed to fall off the cliff, only I didn't die."

Martha stared at her.

"Everyone said Cynthia was clumsy because she was pregnant," Josephine added.

"The baby...?"

"Oh, it died, too. Inside her, I mean. She was only about six months along."

The Garrards had an unpleasant history of accidents, Martha thought. Had she been meant to have an "accident," too? To fall from the cliff while she was drugged?

"Miss Eccles slipped on the stairs, just like Cynthia," Josephine said. "She was lucky to only break a leg."

Sarah edged into the room. "You went someplace two days in a row," she said accusingly, glowering at Martha. "You didn't even ask me if I wanted to go on the boat yesterday, and neither did Charn. I thought you were going to be my friend."

"I am," Martha said. "And next time I go anywhere, I'll see if you can come, too. After all, Josephine didn't go with me, either, so you shouldn't be angry."

"Cathleen says I can come to the party for a while tomorrow, but I know Aunt Natalie will make me go to bed early and I'll miss most of it," Sarah complained.

Why didn't Jules send this child to school, where she'd have other children her age to make friends with? It was monstrous, shutting her up in that house. Martha wondered if she could tackle Jules about finding a school for Sarah.

"Jo, what are you reading?" Sarah asked. "Will you read to me?"

"Not this. You're too young for Sylvia Plath."

Martha eyed the slim white volume in Josephine's lap. *Ariel*. Johann had liked Plath. "She's right, you know," Martha remembered him saying. "Dying *is* an art, the greatest challenge for any human. Not the phony staggering around clutching at one's chest and then delivering a three-minute monologue—not a stage death. But dying. Going out with style."

"I thought Plath stuck her head in an oven," Martha had said.

Johann had flung *Ariel* across the room, crying, "You can't understand the simplest abstraction! God save me from Capricorns!"

When Martha went to her own room, Sarah was sitting in Josephine's lap, the two of them on the floor, and Josephine was teaching her a song about the wind, which she said she'd learned when she was a girl in school.

After dinner that evening, Martha made her way quietly along the corridor leading to Norman Garrard's quarters. She kept an eye out for Natalie, not wishing to upset her again. What an odd match, Matthew and Natalie. She had married late in life, according to Josephine, and Matthew was certainly younger than she. It was hard to think of any man falling in love with the formidable Natalie. Yet Matthew certainly seemed to care for her.

In Norman's room Martha found Simon helping the old man drink orange juice. "Hello, Mr. Garrard," she said, deliberately not speaking to Simon. "Are you feeling well enough for a visitor?"

Simon put down the glass and hurried toward her.

"What're you doing in here?" he muttered as he came close. "Mr. G. didn't ask you. . . ."

Martha ignored him and went to the bedside.

" 'Evening," Norman said. He caught Simon's eye and motioned for him to go out.

Simon stood his ground for a moment, glaring at Martha. Then he shrugged and obeyed.

"I wanted to ask you where you found Josephine. She thinks it was Oregon." Martha grasped the hand that groped toward her, feeling his thready pulse under her fingers.

"Malville. Inland. Farm. People named Reynolds. Thought the woman knew. Something. Wouldn't tell me. Offered money. Nothing. Brought Josephine back here. Take care."

"I will. But how did she get to Oregon?"

He shook his head. Oxygen bubbled through the water bottle on the tank and into the old man's nose. His lips were blue.

"Does Jules. . . ?" she began, and then saw Norman's eyes widen and look past her.

She turned. Jules stood in the doorway.

"I hardly think my father's in any shape to have you visit him daily," Jules said.

"That's what I told her," Simon said from behind Jules. He stalked toward the bed. "She walks in here like she owned the place, and I said—"

"Please come downstairs," Jules said to Martha.

She followed him.

When they were in the library, he closed the door and sat behind the desk, stranding her on the other side. "What's your business with my father?" he asked.

"Josephine," she said bluntly. "He knows where she was. He brought her back to Victoria."

"Who told you that?"

"He did. He sent for me yesterday and told me. I went back today to find out more if I could—Natalie interrupted yesterday. He—your father—won't talk if there's anyone else around. He says nobody knows but him."

"That's true. What else did he tell you?"

"Just that he wanted me to—to keep Josephine safe."

"So you said yesterday."

"He says she's not crazy. Jules, why is everyone in the house so—strange about Josephine? Cathleen treats her like a child, Charn teases or ignores her and you—punish her."

"Punish her?" Jules's voice rose.

"You keep her a virtual prisoner in this house. She's immature—she *does* react childishly—but no one's allowing her to grow up. She needs people her age, something to do...."

"She won't see her friends."

"Oh, Jules, she doesn't have any friends after all this time—she's too far removed now from those girls she went to school with."

"What would you suggest I do?"

"Bran Lowrey offered to take both Josephine and me on a sightseeing excursion. I think it would do her good, and surely with two of us to look after her...."

"I'll consider it."

"Then maybe next semester Josephine and I could go together to a class or two at the university. Something like that."

Jules sighed. "I wish I could be as optimistic as you are," he said.

"Stasis solves nothing," she told him. "I'm sorry if I've troubled you by seeing your father, but I certainly know enough not to endanger his life."

"I should have known a redhead would demand action."

Martha touched her hair. "Oh, I'm not really," she said.

"Blond Marty Collier," the papers had called her.

"A red-gold," Jules insisted. "You have lovely hair."

"Thank you." She heard the stiffness in her words. But he'd been the one to put the desk between them, reminding her that she was his employee. Still, it warmed her that he liked her hair. Johann had insisted that she become a blonde for him....

"Martha...."

She looked up and met Jules's eyes. Her breath caught.

The door flew open. "Aha—there you are!" Cathleen whirled into the room and perched on the desk. "Jules, I absolutely must have both Henry and Bill for at least an hour this evening or the treasure hunt will be a total failure."

"Can I help?" Martha asked politely.

Cathleen looked at her. "Why—I imagine you can. Help me round up the men and we'll see."

Once they had left the library and were crossing the foyer, Cathleen grasped Martha's arm. "If you know what's good for you, you'll leave Jules alone," she said.

"I'm not—"

"Don't come over all smarmy with me like you do with him. I'm no fool. I can tell what you're up to. Stay away from him if you want to stay at Black Tor."

CHAPTER THIRTEEN

AFTER CATHLEEN STALKED OFF, Martha went upstairs and continued reading the Garrard family history.

She found that Norman's mother had also died in an accident. A streetcar had been crossing the Point Ellice Bridge on a May afternoon in 1896, when a rotten beam in the center span of the bridge gave way and the streetcar plunged into the water below. Amanda Garrard was one of the passengers who perished. What she was doing on the streetcar without her husband or son was not mentioned. It seemed odd to Martha—surely with Abel's wealth Amanda would have had her own carriage.

At least everyone had been sure of her death, unlike Abel's twin sisters, who were "presumably lost overboard" while on a boat bound for Vancouver. Or the Garrard cousin—again female—who was "missing from her room one morning and was never again seen on the face of this earth."

Is that what Josephine had meant when she'd said there were others like her? Was there a sinister quirk in the Garrard heritage—a darkness that settled over the mind? For certainly the tendency toward a certain type of mental illness was inherited.

Martha's attention strayed from the book and she found herself wondering about Miss Eccles's accident. Josephine's former nurse suspected that she hadn't merely fallen on the stairs.

I could go and see her, Martha thought. *She's right here in Victoria, in St. Joseph's Hospital.* Jules might not approve, but he needn't know. Jules. Martha sighed. She didn't need Cathleen's warning to realize that she should avoid him. Not that Cathleen had the right. . . .

Martha closed the book sharply.

The party was the following day. She wasn't looking forward to it at all. Parties were a reminder of the bad times with Johann; toward the last, his parties had been demonic nightmares.

But presumably there'd be no overt sex at a party held at Black Tor. Jules wasn't the kind of man to permit it.

Why do I find him so fascinating? she asked herself. *Must I always choose badly? He's a dangerous man. He could be hoping to gain control of Josephine's share of their inheritance. Would that be so very difficult? Have Josephine committed to a mental hospital—be declared her guardian. What choice more natural than her brother? But, then, why try to kill Josephine?*

However the next morning, when Jules invited her to visit Butchart Gardens, she accepted without any hesitation, all dark thoughts of him firmly pushed to the back of her mind.

"Josephine's caught up in the party plans," he said. "This may be your last outing for—well, for some time." He frowned. "I'd like to think she won't descend into her usual depression afterward, but I'm not an optimist. Besides, *I'd* like to take you somewhere."

She wrenched her eyes from his. "I'd love to go," she said. "Bran told me the gardens are unbelievable." She thrust Bran's name between them deliberately, but Jules seemed not to notice.

How does Jules feel about me? Martha asked herself. *Was there no love in his kiss, in his embrace? Does he see me as a Nida, to be conquered by sex? Has he known all along about Marty Collier?*

But none of it mattered. She wanted to go with him, and she felt a flare of satisfaction as she thought of Cathleen's annoyance.

"We'll go after lunch," Jules said.

Martha found Josephine on the back terrace with Cathleen and Sarah. Sarah ran over to her and took her hand. "They aren't going to let me help in the treasure hunt tonight!" she complained.

"You know very well you aren't allowed outside after dark," Cathleen told Sarah.

"Don't be sulky," Josephine added. "Aunt Natalie would never let you, even if we said you could."

"But I'll miss all the fun!" Sarah wailed. She tugged at Martha's hand. "Can't you make them let me?"

"It's not my party," Martha said. "And if the treasure hunt is to be after dark, then I think probably you should—"

"Oh—you're as bad as they are!" Sarah cried. Then she ran from the terrace, across the lawn, and disappeared behind a privet hedge.

Martha hesitated, then started after the girl.

"She's spoiled," Cathleen said. "Always gets her own way. Just ignore her—she'll get over it."

Spoiled? A child for whom no one seemed to take direct responsibility? Martha walked across the neatly clipped grass. When she came to the hedge, she peered around, but there was no sign of Sarah. A man bending over a flower bed glanced up when she appeared.

"Have you seen Sarah—the little girl?" she asked.

He stood up. "She ran past me but I don't know where she went."

Martha noted his Oriental features. "Are you Bill Wong?" she asked.

He nodded.

"Then you're the one who took the note for Josephine the other day. Sarah said a man gave you the note."

He looked at her, saying nothing.

"Could you describe the man? Have you ever seen him before. Do you know who he is?" Martha asked.

Bill Wong shook his head.

"You can't even describe him?"

He shrugged. "Didn't pay any attention," he said.

"Well, was he tall? Short?"

"I couldn't say, miss." Bill knelt beside the roses and began digging around their roots with a cultivator fork, dismissing her.

Martha controlled her annoyance and walked on past him to the edge of the woods. "Sarah!" she called.

The trees were huge trunked, with their branches meeting overhead to darken the paths between them.

"Sarah!" she called again, not eager to venture into the gloom.

"What do you want?"

Martha started as the girl seemed to materialize in front of her. "I thought maybe we could talk."

"What about?" Sarah's eyes were red, but she'd stopped crying. "You don't really like me, either. Nobody does."

"I do like you," Martha said. "How can you find your way about in the woods? I'm afraid I'd be lost in no time."

"It used to be a grove," Sarah said. "But then they let the trees go wild. Most of the time I like the woods. I don't *really* believe Ahlmakoh lives in there. That's for babies."

"Ahlmakoh—the woods spirit?"

"That's right. Ahlmakoh's sort of a bad spirit who lives in the woods. He can be real fierce and mean."

"Does your Uncle Matthew tell you lots of stories about the Indian spirits?" Martha asked.

"Some. There's the Yaai. They live on mountaintops and disappear like fog. Only they're little and can sort of fly like fairies. He says maybe they're the ghosts of little girls."

Ghosts of little girls? Martha thought. *Isn't that rather gloomy to be telling a child?* "I don't know your Uncle Matthew very well," Martha said to Sarah.

"He talks to me sometimes. I like him better than Aunt Natalie. But Uncle Norman's the best of all. I'm sorry he's going to die."

"Do you have any friends to play with around here?" Martha asked.

"I used to play with Jimmy Smithson sometimes—Bill Wong is his grandfather. But Aunt Natalie made Bill stop bringing him here."

When they neared the terrace, Sarah darted away from Martha and went around toward the front of the house. Martha climbed the steps to rejoin Cathleen and Josephine.

"Well, is she over her sulks?" Cathleen asked.

"More or less," Martha said. "I've wondered why she isn't sent off to school—it seems so lonesome for her out here. No other children. . . ."

Cathleen shrugged. "That's Jules's stiff neck." She smiled narrowly. "You don't know him very well."

"Oh, Martha's half in love with him just like you are," Josephine said. "For all the good that will do either of you. He's like Grandpa Abel—he'll never marry again until he gets old. Daddy was like that, too. And he shouldn't have married my mother. He never loved her at all."

"What are you making?" Martha asked, hoping to change the subject. She picked up one of the small packets bound with red ribbon that lay on the table.

"Oh, we can't tell you—it's part of the treasure hunt," Josephine said. "Only Cathleen and I know."

Thus dismissed, Martha entered the house. *I must talk to Jules about Sarah,* she thought. *We could take her with us today, at least. I could say Josephine and Cathleen don't want her underfoot—which is true enough.*

When Jules and Martha drove away in the MG after lunch, Sarah was with them.

"I thought this was Charn's car," Martha said.

"The cars belong to the estate," Jules said. "My father wanted—wants—it that way."

That means what? Martha wondered. *That Norman Garrard owns everything?* "Is there a family business?" she asked.

"Not any longer. Investments, mostly. My father inherited old Abel's penchant for selling out at the right time. We don't own anything outright, not now."

They passed through fields of flowers, gold and bronze, and then an expanse of pure scarlet that made Martha catch her breath.

"Salvia," Jules said. "Flower growing is one of Victoria's industries. Do you know anything about Butchart Gardens?"

"It used to be a quarry," Sarah offered. "They took all this rock out and left a big hole, and Mrs. Butchart couldn't stand seeing it so ugly and so she planted lots of trees and flowers and things to make it beautiful, and it is."

"Couldn't have told the story better myself," Jules said wryly. "September isn't the ideal month to see the gardens, but they *are* fabulous at any season."

Hanging baskets of geraniums lined the drive in the parking lot. They left the car and wandered down paths that threaded between flowers of every color, shrubs and exotic trees.

Martha didn't recognize half of the plantings she saw, and though Jules murmured St. John's wort or Japanese hydrangea vine as they passed, she couldn't take everything in. She felt drunk with color. "How many years did this all take?" she asked.

"Well, of course the family did live here at the time this

was begun. I think the Ross Fountain—he's the grandson—was put in in 1964," Jules said, "and that was the sixtieth anniversary. So they're past the diamond jubilee."

"Black Tor's older than that," Sarah said loyally. "Only they didn't spend so much time planting flowers."

"There's a night tour with illumination," Jules said. "I'd like to bring you back again sometime."

"Oh, here's the Japanese Garden!" Sarah cried. "My very favorite of all." She ran ahead to cross the stepping-stones over a small stream and climb on the bridge.

"She's alone too much," Martha said to Jules. "In the house with no other children around."

"I suppose she is," Jules said slowly. "But for now...."

She waited, but he didn't continue. "Isn't there a school she could attend?" she asked.

"Norman wants her at Black Tor," he said. "My father is still head of the household. Actually, Louella is an excellent teacher. She—"

"Sarah needs companionship," Martha said. "She doesn't even have Jimmy Smithson to play with anymore."

"Who?"

"Bill Wong's grandson."

"I didn't even know he had a grandson Sarah's age, much less that she knew him."

"You don't care about Sarah, that's why," Martha said, keeping her voice down with an effort. "No one seems to. She's well fed and clothed and even educated, but no one really *cares* about her."

"You do, evidently."

"Yes. She needs—she needs love."

"Don't we all?" Jules said softly.

She turned her head and saw how he was looking at her, and felt the pulse in her neck throb.

"Let's see if the kittens are in the arbor," Sarah said, appearing beside them, and the moment was over.

They stopped at a refreshment stand because Sarah wanted a hamburger to feed the kittens. Martha and Jules had a cup of tea as they sat on a bench in an ivy-covered arbor. A gray kitten with a white vest poked his head out from the shrubbery and ventured toward the bits of meat Sarah was crumbling on the ground.

"There're always kittens around here," Jules said.

"But none at Black Tor," Martha reminded him. "You don't have any animals there."

"No," said Jules. "No pets."

"That's a shame. Sarah would enjoy—"

"The only animals at Black Tor are stuffed," Jules said. "And that's how it has to stay."

CHAPTER FOURTEEN

WHEN THEY RETURNED TO THE HOUSE, Martha went to her room to freshen up. She found Josephine searching through her dresser drawers. "What are you looking for?" she asked, startled and annoyed.

"The coral necklace, of course," Josephine said impatiently. "You'll have to wear it tonight. You haven't lost the coral, have you? Because then you'll be completely unprotected. I—"

"Whatever are you talking about?" Martha pulled open the drawer of her nightstand and removed the coral necklace. "I keep it here," she said.

Josephine hurried over, snatched the coral from Martha's hands and tried to fasten it around Martha's neck. But she was unable to work the clasp, and Martha reached up to hook the necklace herself.

"There, I have it on," she said. "Now what's this all about?"

"I didn't really forget about the cliff," Josephine said. "Only with Diego coming back and all, I didn't pay enough attention. You couldn't have pulled the blanket over. I know. I was drugged, too, that other time, and you just collapse. If you try to move, it takes minutes to make your arm obey. You didn't drag the blanket to the edge, but there you were. So I know you're in danger now like I am. Only I'm not sure if there's one person or more, and I can't help you much because I don't know who—"

"Why would I be in danger?" Martha asked.

"Because of me. If you're gone, I'll be alone. They won't get another nurse if something happens to you. Aunt Natalie didn't want another nurse after Miss Eccles fell on the stairs, but she was sick for a while and Jules hired you, anyway. They don't know about Diego, though. They don't know I can get away now."

"Who are 'they'?"

"I told you, I don't know for sure."

"Why didn't they just push me over while I was drugged?" Martha asked. "I wasn't hurt at all, actually."

"I think Sarah came back too soon," Josephine said. "And they had to leave so she wouldn't see them. The blanket was dragged over with you on it, and then you were supposed to be tipped over the cliff with the blanket left on the edge to show how careless you'd been. Something like that."

Martha shivered. Was she being told what Josephine had meant to do herself? She fingered the coral around her neck.

"It's a talisman," Josephine said. "I told you the first time I saw the necklace. Coral protects against peril. Don't take if off. Please. And don't trust anyone but me. And Sarah." Josephine gazed at her steadily. "I can feel danger around both of us. I can almost see it like a poisonous cloud. Don't wear green tonight."

"Why not?"

"Green is unlucky. We can't afford to be unlucky. I never wear green. Do you have anything yellow?"

Yellow? Martha thought. With the coral necklace? Some color combination! But she probably should humor Josephine's superstitions. "I have a yellow top," she said. "But why yellow?"

"Evil spirits are afraid of yellow."

"Evil spirits? Like Ahlmakoh? I—"

"Don't you think whoever plans to harm you is evil?"

Josephine said. "I'm not afraid of Uncle Matthew's Indian monsters like Sarah is sometimes, but people are evil, too."

"Where did you learn all this about amulets and unlucky colors?"

Josephine bit her lip. "It's from the two years."

"Did someone tell you stories like Matthew tells Sarah?"

Josephine shook her head. "I don't remember. But these aren't—superstitions. I came back to Black Tor knowing about evil and the ways to turn it aside. I learned in the—lost years. But I don't remember who taught me."

Josephine took a deep breath and sighed. "That's all over now." She smiled at Martha. "Diego is here. He isn't dead. And the party's tonight." Suddenly she twirled away from Martha's side and danced about the room.

Did she really equate the party and Diego's return from the dead? Were they of equal importance to Josephine? Martha wondered. In many ways her emotional maturity seemed to be fixed at sixteen.

"Shall we rest awhile before we dress for the party?" Martha asked.

"Oh, I couldn't. But I'll try to read."

"Sylvia Plath?"

"Oh, no, no—I'll read some more about Emily Carr. She came out on top in spite of everything. She fought. I can, too, now that I have something to fight for."

The party began slowly, but the punch was potent, and soon everyone was talking and laughing. Bran arrived and headed for Martha, but he was quickly intercepted by Cathleen.

"She wants all the men," Josephine said, scowling. She wore a silver pants ensemble with brilliant yellow beads and sandals to match. "I'll have to wait to meet him, I suppose. Cathleen looks like she intends to keep him all night."

Charn came up from behind and put an arm around each of them. "The two most beautiful girls at the party," he said. "Like day and night. Marty's the sunny morning in her yellow shirt, and Josie's the silvery twilight."

Martha froze.

"I *hate* that nickname," Josephine said. "I'm not Josie and never will be."

Martha tried to relax. *Charn means nothing,* she assured herself. *He doesn't know about Marty Collier.*

But he might. He could have been the man in her room that night. She didn't know for sure it had been Simon. . . .

"Ready or not!" Cathleen shouted above the hubbub. "Game time."

There were mixed groans and cheers.

"It's my party and I make the rules," Cathleen said. "We're going to have an old-fashioned treasure hunt. With a twist. You'll find out later what *that* will be. Right now Ruth is passing a tray with beribboned packets to all the men, while Francis is doing the same for the women. Match ribbon colors for your partners. Then open your packets and follow the clues. Flashlights for all on the terrace. Good hunting!"

Martha found herself matched with Charn.

"I bribed Ruth and Francis to give us the same color," he said.

"Oh?"

"Otherwise, when do I see you?"

"I spent a day fishing with you, as I recall."

"You've spent as much time since with Jules and with that museum fellow, Bran Lowrey. Where did you meet him?"

"On the ferry coming over."

Charn smiled. "Then he's not an old friend?"

"Certainly not." Martha opened her packet and read it aloud:

"Dimple in chin
Devil within."

"I think I know..." Charn began, then opened his own and read:

> "The arrow flies
> The orca dies.

"Yes, I'm right," he said. "The first clue is easy—come on, let's hurry."

He took Martha's hand and led her around the side of the house to a small formal garden, where a fountain sprayed water from a stone statue of Eros.

"See, he's Cupid—a dimple in his chin, and the arrow is roughly pointed at the whale on top of the tower," Charn said.

"But where's the next clue?" Martha asked.

"Somewhere close." He played the flashlight over the pool of water and they both saw the cork floater at the same moment. A piece of paper wrapped in water-proofing was attached to it with a nylon line and lead sinker.

> "A rose is a rose
> Right under your nose."

Charn read the clue aloud and they stared at each other.

"The rose garden?" Martha asked.

"Too obvious."

"I—I suppose Josephine is all right," she said. "I didn't see who her partner was."

"Jules saw to that," Charn said. "He's her partner—he made Cathleen set it up that way."

"Oh, well, then...."

"I've an idea," Charn said, leading her to the music room, where he pointed out a painting of a plump, red-cheeked child with a basket of flowers, roses among them. The girl had the basket lifted, and her head was bent over the blossoms. Behind the frame Charn found a riddle that he was also able to decipher.

The next clue was harder, and they made two false stops before they found a paper. It read:

Chestnuts enfold
The ruins old.

Chestnuts, Martha thought. The woods. She would have hung back, but Charn had her hand and was hurrying her along toward the grove. The evening dimness had deepened into true dark.

"Old Cath can really think up the damndest stunts," he was saying. "I wonder what she's got rigged. She wouldn't tell me anything."

"In the woods?" Martha asked.

"There's an ancient summerhouse there. Falling apart."

Their flashlights made round holes of light in the darkness under the trees. Martha pulled against Charn's urging.

"What's the matter? Scared?"

"No, not really."

"I can cure that," he said, stopping and putting his arms around her.

His mouth came down on hers, warm; his hands pulled her body against his. She tried to push him away. "You know I want you, Marty," he said, his voice husky. "Why pretend? You want me, too, I know you do because I know who you are. Cath told me."

Martha managed to free herself and ran from him, stumbling on roots and dropping her flashlight. She heard him curse and then call her name. She groped for the flashlight, but the fall had put it out and she couldn't find it. She went on more slowly, unable to see where she was going. At last she stopped and looked around at the darkness. There were other voices, faint. Something rustled nearby, and a bird screeched. She clutched at the tree trunk next to her and swallowed against rising panic.

I'm not lost, she told herself. But the woods felt menacing in the blackness, and she had no idea which way to go. Her hand went up to touch the coral necklace hidden under her yellow shirt.

I can't be in any danger, she thought. *If I call out, they'll find me. Who? Charn? He knows I'm Marty Collier. I don't want Charn near me. What did he say—Cathleen had told him? If she knows. . . .*

Martha rested her forehead against the tree. Jules would know, too. He would probably ask her to leave.

Something scuttled under her feet, and she cried out and jumped away. Her momentary fright started her moving, but she had no direction and blundered into trees and stumbled repeatedly. Tears filled her eyes. The darkness seemed to be actively against her, and her heart beat rapidly as fear prickled along her spine.

At last there was a glow ahead, and she hurried toward the light as fast as she could, coming out finally into a small clearing. But she wasn't back at the house. Flame flickered in dozens of hurricane lamps, some strung on tree branches and some on the veranda of a small building she'd never seen before. As Martha moved closer, she heard someone laugh. Then she saw people gathered by a table on the porch. Was this the summerhouse?

"Ah, another straggler," someone said.

A figure came toward her.

Martha shrank back but was afraid to plunge into the darkness, and there was nowhere else to go.

"Martha."

Jules's voice. She swayed toward him, then caught herself.

"What's the matter?" Jules asked.

She put a hand up to her disheveled hair, her scratched face. "I—I got lost."

As she spoke, Charn burst into the light, calling her

name. She clutched at Jules's sleeve. He put his arm around her.

"There you are. That was a dumb thing to do, you know." Charn's tone was harsh. "Scared me to death after I saw you drop the flashlight. You could have hurt yourself."

Martha couldn't answer. People approached, curious.

"Are you sure she wasn't running away from you?" Jules asked.

Someone laughed.

"I guess she has *your* number, old buddy," a man's voice said.

"Is everyone here now?" a voice called—Cathleen's voice. "Then let's gather round. Refreshments are available for flagging spirits, and speaking of spirits...." She paused and turned toward the door leading into the unlighted interior of the summerhouse.

There was a short silence. Then the door slowly opened and a figure wearing a long dark robe emerged. A hood covered the head, and the face was shadowed.

The robed figure drifted onto the porch and down the few steps to the ground, then moved toward a mound near the far edge of the clearing, where a bonfire had been lit. Blue flames flared and crackled.

In a deep voice the figure intoned, "The devil rides the blue flame and He is among us. Form the circle."

"Around the fire," Cathleen ordered, her voice shrill. "Quickly, everyone, a circle around the fire! Hold hands—find your partner and hold hands, man, woman, around the circle."

Jules started toward the fire, bringing Martha with him.

"Jules," she said, "I don't want to." The whole scene filled her with horror.

"Don't be upset—this is just Cathleen's fakery."

Martha swallowed the bile in her throat. The cowled figure and the blue-flamed fire were a repetition of a scene from Johann's *The Unmasking of Hell*. The circle of sycophants—everything. Cathleen had planned this. For her. For Marty Collier.

CHAPTER FIFTEEN

MARTHA HAD CAUGHT a glimpse or two of Bran during the evening. Now she saw him watching her from the partially formed circle, Cathleen's hand in his. Did he know, too? Did everyone know she had been Marty Collier?

There was no place to run. Jules, holding her right hand, pulled her into the circle. Then someone else took her left hand. She glanced to the left and saw it was Charn, and her muscles tensed, but his grasp was firm. Now the circle was complete. Josephine stood to the other side of Jules.

The hooded figure in the center began chanting in a ghastly travesty of the warlock scene from *The Unmasking of Hell*:

> Lord Asmodeus
> Demon of dark lore,
> We, your worshippers
> Bring blood to your altar....

The circle moved widdershins, slowly at first, picking up speed as the chant grew faster.

Martha clenched her teeth. Soon, soon now, the warlock would throw back his hood and point his finger to bring Nida forth from the others....

The cowl fell from the head of the robed figure, and she stared at the white-haired man inside the circle. It was Matthew, Natalie's husband.

Martha felt a drag on her right hand; the circle slowed.

"All right, everyone—refreshments and prizes." Jules's voice, not Cathleen's.

The circle broke up. Martha pulled her hand from Charn's and went to Josephine's side. Cathleen strode past her toward Jules.

"I wasn't finished—we didn't get to the best part. You promised me—"

"I did no such thing," Jules said. "I told you anything in good taste, and this was rapidly passing that point. I certainly hope you hadn't intended to go on with the rest of that ugly scene. And you, Matthew."

Matthew, who had come up behind Martha, spread his hands. "Actually, the original work—the novel—was quite authentic," he said. "Collier perverted it for the movie, to appeal to prurient tastes, but the book—"

"I found the movie offensive," Jules said. "I've never read the book. Cathleen told me she wanted folk dancing tonight." He raised his voice. "Back to the house!" he called to the crowd.

"Honestly, Jules, you're such a stick sometimes," Cathleen said.

"But not a liar," he told her.

Most of the people had drifted past them and into the woods, heading for the house. Flashlights bobbed among the trees.

"No more liar than she is—your precious nurse who calls herself Martha Jamison." Cathleen jerked her head at Martha. "Ask *her* about the movie, about Johann Collier. She ought to know—she was his wife! She's Marty Collier!"

The few remaining people looked at Martha. She saw the yellow glint of reflected fire in Jules's eyes and spoke only to him.

"I *am* Martha Jamison," she said. "I resumed my maiden name. I was Johann Collier's wife, yes. I'd like to forget it. The past was—very painful."

Matthew spoke first. "Personally, I never believed you guilty," he said.

"Guilty of what?" Josephine asked.

"The newspapers hinted of irregularities in Johann Collier's death," Matthew said. "Scandal sheets—that's all they are."

"I don't remember much about it," Josephine said. "Didn't he commit suicide?"

"The police decided he had," Matthew said. "They—"

"I believe you should rejoin your guests, Cathleen," Jules cut in. "It's rude to keep them waiting."

"Martha told me she'd been married," Josephine said. "She didn't lie to me. What do I care who she was married to? What difference does it make?"

Cathleen put an arm over Josephine's shoulders. "Now that we know who Martha is, we also know what kind of person she is. Hardly fit to care for an innocent like you, Josie."

"I'm *not* Josie! Don't you call me that!" Josephine flung off Cathleen's arm and looked about the clearing, her eyes wide and distraught.

Jules took Josephine's arm. "We're going back to the house," he said. Then he glanced at the group left under the flickering lanterns. "Charn, you lead and I'll bring up the rear so no one will lose their way."

Martha hurried to her room as soon as they reached the house. She closed her door and sat on the bed. Would Jules want her to leave immediately? Was there a way off the island at night?

Jules hadn't looked at or spoken to her after learning that she was Marty Collier. He saw it as deception, pure and simple. *I'm Martha Jamison,* she said to herself. *Always. I tried to be what Johann wanted—Marty. But I couldn't be. I was just Martha, after all.*

Josephine burst into the room.

"Oh, please don't go away from Black Tor, Martha!" she cried. She sat on the bed Indian fashion and touched

Martha's arm. "I know how you don't want to be Marty—why you didn't want to say you were. Cathleen was mean to tell like she did in front of everybody. She's jealous because of Jules. But I need you here. I need one friend. Please, Martha...."

"I think whether I stay is up to Jules, don't you?" Martha said. "After all, he may feel I shouldn't be your companion."

"That's silly," Josephine said.

But Josephine didn't remember what the newspapers had hinted—that Marty Collier was the model for the depraved Nida.

Martha smiled wanly at her. "Why don't you go down and join the party," she suggested. "You'll miss the prizes and—"

"I don't care about Cathleen's old party," Josephine said. "She thinks she's so irresistible, anyway, hanging on to your—your friend Bran so he couldn't even speak to you tonight."

Had Bran been in the group who had heard Cathleen denounce her? Martha wondered. She hadn't noticed; all she'd seen was Jules's set face, cold and unfriendly. Josephine had been there and Charn. And Matthew....

"I was surprised to see your Uncle Matthew as the—in that costume tonight," Martha said. "He seems so quiet."

"Oh, Cathleen probably told him it was to educate everyone about folklore or old customs or something like that. He's sort of a fanatic about those things." She giggled. "Aunt Natalie will be furious when she finds out."

She stared at Martha. "What was that movie all about? Sex and witchcraft?"

Martha nodded. "More or less. My—Johann wasn't quite...well. He wasn't normal. He saw life as he portrayed it in *The Unmasking of Hell*. Distorted."

Josephine grimaced. "He sounds awful. No wonder you don't want to be Marty Collier."

Not awful, Martha thought, but before she could say anything there was a knock at the door and Jules came in.

"Please go to your room, Josephine," he said.

"I want Martha to stay at Black Tor," she told him quickly.

Martha touched Josephine's arm. "Do what your brother says, Josephine. Please."

Josephine got up from the bed and went to the door, giving Jules a black look as she passed him. He shut the door behind her.

Martha remained seated on the bed. He stood over her in silence.

"You could have told me," he said at last.

She shook her head. "You wouldn't have hired me." She nervously fingered the coral necklace under her shirt.

"I'd like you to stay on until I can make—other arrangements," he said.

"Of course." She didn't look at him.

"Martha...I must apologize for tonight's—performance. I had no idea Cathleen meant to—" He broke off.

"Expose me?" she asked, her words clipped. "Perhaps it was for the best. At least now I'm sure it wasn't you who...." Too late, she realized what she was saying.

"What wasn't me?"

"The first night I was at Black Tor, a man came into my room—I hadn't locked my door—and he tried to...." She rose from the bed, walked to her dresser and unhooked the coral necklace. "He thought I would let him—make love to me because he knew I was Marty Collier. I screamed and reached for the light, and he ran. I never did see who he was. I decided later it was probably Simon, but I never did know for sure. After that I kept my door locked at night."

"And you thought I...?"

Martha turned to face Jules. "I didn't really know who the man was," she told him. "So I said nothing. I understand why you want me to leave Black Tor. But I want you to understand me, too. I'm not—not Nida, not the heroine of Johann's movie. I never was."

He grasped her arms.

"Please, Jules," she said.

"I want you," he told her. "I've felt you respond to me."

"Let me go. Please." Tears filled her eyes.

"You could stay in Victoria," he said. "I'd—"

"No!" she cried, twisting from him. "Go away! You're like all the rest—you're like Johann. You want to believe I'm Nida—a windup sex doll. And I'm not, I'm not! Go away, oh, go away!"

He stared at her for a moment, then turned and left the room. She locked the door behind him, threw herself on the bed and cried until she was exhausted. Then, numbed, she changed into her nightgown and crawled under the covers.

She dreamed of Bran, with his brown beard blowing in the ocean breeze. But when she looked at him again she saw it was Jules, instead; Jules with his grandfather's beard—with old Abel's beard. Jules against the gray sea, the two of them on a boat that rocked in choppy waters. The black fin of a killer whale followed the boat, and every so often the black-and-white head would pop up for a look and smile the sinister smile....

Someone was knocking on her door. Martha's eyes flew open to daylight.

"Are you all right? Martha—let me in." Josephine's voice.

She got out of bed and unlocked the door, still bemused by her dream. Was that why she'd dreamed of old Abel before she'd seen his picture? Combining Bran and Jules?

"I heard you crying last night," Josephine said.

"I'm all right now," Martha told her.

"Are you—did Jules say . . . ?"

"I'm going to be here for a little while, anyway." *Let Jules explain to his sister.*

"I went downstairs for a while last night," Josephine said. "Cathleen was nasty to everybody and the party broke up early. The people who were going to stay at Black Tor went to the Empress, instead. Bran told me to tell you he was coming by to pick us up about ten this morning and we'd have lunch out."

"But Jules. . . ."

"Bran said he asked Jules before the party and Jules thought it would be a nice outing." Josephine made a face.

Martha thought of the scene with Jules in her room and the earlier nastiness of the circle in the clearing. She wanted to be away from Black Tor and its people. Except for Josephine.

"All right, let's plan to go," she agreed. "Did Bran say where?"

"He said he'd surprise us."

Sarah ran into the room and jumped on the bed, bouncing. "What's a surprise?" she said.

Josephine looked at Sarah for a moment, then at Martha. "Maybe we could—take her along?" she asked.

Martha hesitated. Josephine's glance had been calculating. Did she intend to run off and see her mysterious Diego while they were out that day, hoping that Sarah would distract both Martha and Bran?

"We'll have to see," Martha said. "Maybe."

"I saw Uncle Matthew last night," Sarah said. "He was dressed in a costume. I asked him if he was a monk, but he said he was a sorcerer. Then I asked him if he could call Shishchuikul out of the mountain, and he said he could."

"Who's that?" Martha asked.

"Shishchuikul? Oh, he's sort of a monster who lives inside the mountain. He's got red hair. Only really bright red. Not like yours, Martha."

Josephine laughed. "You've been listening to Uncle Matthew's Indian stories again. I don't know how you remember all the names. You ought to tell them to Bran today. He'd like to hear about Shishchuikul, I'll bet."

"Are we going out with Bran? The one who took Martha on the tallyho?"

"Yes."

"Oh."

"Don't you like him?" Josephine asked.

"Maybe he won't want to take me," Sarah said.

"Why not?"

"Oh, just because."

"You're silly," Josephine told her. "Don't you want to go?"

"Oh, yes, I do want to."

Martha watched the two of them and felt her throat constrict. *I'll miss Sarah, too,* she thought. *Josephine and Sarah. They seem almost like my family. Maybe because they feel as displaced as I do.*

"I heard Simon tell Aunt Natalie that Uncle Norman won't last another week," Sarah said. "But how can Simon tell?"

"He's guessing," Josephine said. "But he might be right."

"Does—will Uncle Norman's heart stop beating?" Sarah pressed her hand against her own chest. "I can feel mine inside." Her eyes grew round. "What if my heart stops? Will I die?"

Martha put her arms around Sarah. "Your heart will go on beating for years and years. Your Uncle Norman is old, and his heart's just tired and worn out."

Sarah nodded. "That's what Uncle Norman said. He

told me I had to watch over Josephine because he couldn't anymore. But I forget sometimes, so I'm glad you came, Martha. Uncle Norman is, too. He said you were sensible. He said you wouldn't let anyone railroad Josephine into a place. One of *those* places, he said."

Josephine's tawny eyes stared into Martha's. "Please don't leave Black Tor," she said.

CHAPTER SIXTEEN

JOSEPHINE RECEIVED PERMISSION from Aunt Natalie for Sarah to join them in their outing with Bran.

"Natalie's upset about something," Josephine said. "She hardly listened to me. She probably found out about Uncle Matthew at the party last night."

"Wouldn't he have told her what he was going to do?" Martha asked.

Josephine shook her head. "She never approves of anything. She was a sour old maid too long before she married Matthew."

"Has she always lived at Black Tor?"

"Ever since my mother died. She's run the house, too. Daddy wasn't afraid of her, but he usually let her have her way—it was easier than arguing, he said."

"But when Jules was married, didn't Cynthia...?"

"Cynthia didn't count. Besides, she hated Black Tor. And she was afraid of Natalie. Everyone is. Maybe not Jules, though he humors her. And now that daddy's so sick, she runs him."

"What do you mean 'runs him'?"

Josephine shrugged. "Oh, she takes good care of him. But in her own way. Like having Simon when daddy didn't want a male attendant."

"Is Matthew afraid of her?"

"I suppose so. Although he does go off on his field trips when he wants to. Cynthia liked him. She said he was a romantic. Sarah likes him, too."

"You know, Josephine, Sarah should be in school. She has no friends her own age."

"I know. But then Louella would never come out of her room. You've seen her gliding down the stairs like a ghost. You turn around and she's disappeared. Jules told me that's why he continues to have Louella teach Sarah—if Sarah was sent off to school, Louella would just fade away like she was doing before. She *is* an excellent teacher—Sarah seems to know everything."

"Sarah's a bright child," Martha said, "but children need children."

"I'll be a child for her," Josephine said. She spread her arms and whirled across Martha's bedroom to the window. "I don't have any friends my age, either. Except you, and you're five years older."

And I'll soon be gone, Martha thought. *What will happen to Josephine?*

"Don't you have Diego now?" she asked.

"We have to wait," Josephine said. "I can't leave Black Tor while daddy's still alive. They could get him to change the will—I know they've tried. But daddy trusts me. We talk every day. And Diego has his own reasons for waiting."

"But why can't he come to the house?"

"No!" Josephine cried. "Something bad would happen like before, like the two years... They'd never let Diego and me stay together."

"Why?" Martha asked.

"Because of the money. They've tried to kill me three times. Miss Eccles fell down the stairs because she started to believe me and got suspicious. You listened to me right away and look what happened to you on the picnic by the cliff. We have to be careful...." Josephine sighed. "I don't want to think about it anymore. Bran's coming and we're going to be surprised—we're going to have fun!"

Martha remembered the previous night's unpleasant surprise, but, like Josephine, she didn't want to think about her problems.

Bran arrived on time, and they were down the stairs and out the door almost before he'd had time to park and get out of the car.

"Three beautiful girls," he said. "What did I do to deserve such a pleasant fate?"

"This is Sarah," Martha told him. "We invited her to join us."

Bran bowed slightly. "Charmed," he said.

Sarah smiled shyly, staring at him.

Josephine and Sarah sat in the back of the VW, while Martha climbed in front with Bran.

"Where are we going?" Sarah asked as they drove away from Black Tor.

"To a house even bigger than yours," Bran said. "Craigdarroch Castle." Then he turned to Martha. "We saw the place from Beacon Hill Park, if you remember."

"I know all about Craigdarroch," Sarah said from the back. "Robert Dunsmuir never got to live there because he died before they finished building it. His wife, Joan, lived there all alone for eighteen years, and when she died no one wanted to buy it because it was too big. Aunt Louella told me all about the old places in Victoria."

"The Dunsmuirs must have been millionaires," Martha said.

"Coal," Bran said.

"Here on the island? Coal mines?" Martha's tone was disbelieving.

"The mines are worked out now, but California imported a lot of Vancouver Island coal before the turn of the century. There's even a town called Dunsmuir in California."

They drove up a hill on a street lined with older houses,

and suddenly the castle was before them. Martha was disappointed. Houses crowded to either side made the multichimnied building seem a great gray elephant in a pen.

"The grounds used to be extensive," Bran said. "Twenty acres. But all of it was auctioned off after Joan Dunsmuir died."

They climbed steep stone steps into a paneled entrance hall with a fireplace whose legend read: WELCOME EVER SMILES AND FAREWELL GOES OUT SIGHING.

"The brochure says the castle has a minstrel gallery," Bran said.

"It's for musicians," Sarah explained. "Aunt Louella says they used to sit there and play and you could hear the music all over the house."

As she spoke, music drifted down the stairs—pianos, someone singing a hymn.

"The minstrel gallery?" Martha asked.

"No—the brochure says the Victoria School of Music uses the castle," Bran said.

Every room was paneled in glowing wood. But in the hall and on the stairs where there were no windows, the effect was one of gloom. Martha found the darkness oppressive, and she wondered if Joan Dunsmuir hadn't found it depressing, sitting alone in the castle her husband had built for her.

"The castle's all right," Sarah said as they climbed back into the VW. "I liked the fireplace with the colored windows best, but Black Tor's really nicer to live in."

"I can't imagine living in Craigdarroch," Martha said.

I don't belong at Black Tor, either, she told herself. *I'm not the right person to run a great house and manage servants. Not that Jules ever asked me to. Or would.*

"Now for Point Ellice House," Bran said. "Then, lunch on a beached ship."

The Point Ellice House was more of a museum than anything else, with objects stuffed in every available space. Martha left with a confused impression of multitudes of O'Reillys whose every belonging from swaddling clothes to pictures taken in the coffin had been indiscriminately preserved. Again, the grounds had once been lovely, with green lawns sloping to the river—a river now completely commercial. The place was surrounded by factories and warehouses; log booms floated in the river.

They drove across the Point Ellice bridge, and Martha remembered the earlier bridge collapse where Abel's first wife had died. They passed more manufacturing and lumberyards, then came to the Princess Mary Restaurant.

"Was this a real boat?" Sarah asked.

"Yes," Bran told her.

"I've never been out on a boat," Sarah said. "No one wants to take me. Martha went with Charn and they caught some salmon."

"That's what I plan to have for lunch," Bran said. "I haven't had good salmon for years."

After they'd eaten, Sarah and Martha went to use the bathroom, when they came out, there was no one at their table.

As Martha followed Sarah outside, she saw Bran and Josephine by the car. Josephine was looking up at him, he down at her. Neither of them moved, seemingly frozen in position.

Sarah ran ahead of Martha to the car. Bran turned away from Josephine and smiled at the child, and a flicker of recognition lit the edge of Martha's mind.

"I wish we could stay all day and all night and tomorrow," Josephine said. "I don't want to go back."

The thought, whatever it had been, was gone. Martha climbed into the VW. She didn't want to go back, either.

They drove through town and were approaching the turnoff to Black Tor, when suddenly Bran jammed on the brakes and they were all thrown forward as a panel truck whooshed by.

"Stupid bastard!" Bran exclaimed.

"He almost ran into us!" Sarah cried.

Martha turned to make sure Josephine was all right and her eyes met Josephine's.

"Another try," Josephine said.

"What?" Bran had pulled the VW onto the shoulder. "What do you mean?"

"That truck tried to run you off the road, didn't he?" Josephine asked.

"He came damn close." Bran turned in his seat. "You aren't hurt, are you?" he asked Josephine. "You or Sarah?"

"We're fine. But who was in the truck?"

"A man," Sarah said. "I couldn't see him very well."

"Are you all right, Martha?" Bran asked.

"Yes. Do you think the truck deliberately tried to . . . ?"

"Could have been deliberate." Bran frowned. "What's going on?"

"Please just drive us home, Bran," Josephine said. "I don't want to—to talk about it now. I want to go home."

He started the car, and they reached Black Tor with no further incident.

After they were all out of the car, Josephine swayed against Bran. "I—feel a little faint," she said.

"I'll carry you." He swept her up, and Martha went ahead to open the door.

Josephine insisted that Bran put her down in the foyer, saying she was fine now and Martha could help her up to her room. She leaned on Martha's arm, and they climbed slowly up the stairs. When Josephine was on her bed, Martha checked her pulse and found it regular and strong. She pulled the coverlet over Josephine.

"I'm all right now, I really am. Let me rest until dinner." Josephine closed her eyes.

"I'll sit in here and read," Martha offered.

"Please don't. I feel like you're watching me. I'll call you if I want anything."

"Well...."

"Don't hover over me!" Josephine said irritably, eyes open again. "I can't bear that. Just let me rest. Alone."

"I'll stay in my room, then," Martha said. "I can hear if you—"

"I know you can!" Josephine interrupted. Then she turned her head away.

After a moment Martha went out. She walked to the head of the stairs to see if Bran was still waiting to find out about Josephine, but no one was in the foyer except the killer whale with its enigmatic smile.

In her room Martha took off her shoes and lay on the bed. But she couldn't rest. The horror of the scene in the woods the night before came flooding over her. What would have happened if Jules hadn't stopped the parody? Would she, as Nida, have been dragged before the warlock? Would he have stripped her and—and....

Bile rushed into Martha's mouth and she sat up, afraid she would vomit. She went into the bathroom and washed her face with cold water.

When she went in to check on Josephine, she found her room empty. A piece of paper on the dresser caught Martha's eye. "I'm in the tower," was written in black ink.

Josephine's favorite spot. But should she have tried to climb all those steps if she didn't feel up to par?

Martha hurried across the hall to the tower door and started up the curving staircase. "Josephine!" she called.

No one answered.

She climbed one flight. Another.

"Josephine!"

Silence.

When she came out into the tower room, she found

Sarah crouched on a window seat with playing cards spread out in front of her. Josephine wasn't there.

"Do you want to play crazy eights?" Sarah asked.

"Why didn't you answer when I called?" Martha demanded.

"I'm not Josephine," Sarah said.

"You could have called down and told me she wasn't up here."

"I didn't think about that," Sarah said.

Martha scanned the grounds from the tower windows.

"You remember I told you about the kings and queens and jacks?" Sarah said. "Well, I've decided you're the queen of hearts because—"

Martha heard Sarah's words without comprehension. Where was Josephine? No sign of her outside. But wait—wasn't that Bran's car driving back toward the house?

Martha descended the steps as rapidly as she dared, came out into the upstairs hall and reached the top of the staircase just as Bran brought Josephine into the foyer.

Martha hurried down to them.

"You'd better see what's the matter," Bran said. "I found her running down the driveway—saw her in my rearview mirror. She tried to talk me into taking her into Victoria."

CHAPTER SEVENTEEN

MARTHA LOOKED ABOUT the foyer. Had anyone heard? There was no one in sight. She took Josephine's hand in hers, expecting resistance, argument, but Josephine hung her head and followed her docilely toward the stairs.

"Is there anything I can do?" Bran asked.

Martha looked at him over her shoulder. "No. Just— don't talk about this."

"I won't," he said, and with that he left.

Martha brought Josephine into her bedroom. Josephine sat on the bed, staring at the floor.

"Where were you going?" Martha asked.

"I wanted to see Diego," Josephine said.

"You shouldn't have tried to involve Bran. I'll have to tell Jules, you know that. It'll mean more restrictions for you."

Josephine's head came up and she fixed her eyes on Martha. "Why must you tell Jules? I didn't leave the grounds. Bran saw to that."

"Because my job is to look after you."

"You *do* look after me. Will you believe me if I tell you I won't leave the house again without telling you?" The sherry-colored eyes were wide and pleading. "Please, Martha. I can't stand it if Jules makes me see Dr. Marston right now. I don't like to talk to the doctor—he wants to hypnotize me, and I'm afraid."

"You might remember the past under hypnosis. People have, you know."

Josephine shook her head violently. "I won't let him. Never! I have to keep what I have. You understand, don't you? I know I'm Josephine Garrard and I live at Black Tor and I'm almost twenty-three. I have to hold that knowledge. I'm afraid to have anyone tamper with my mind. What if—if I lost myself again?" She clutched at Martha's hand. "And now I've found Diego again, too. I'd lose him. I couldn't bear that."

"Will you let me meet Diego?"

"If I say yes, will you promise not to tell Jules about today?"

After all, nothing happened, Martha argued to herself. *Bran brought Josephine back quickly. I must meet Diego and find out about him—I'm the only one besides Josephine who knows he exists.* "All right," Martha said. "The next time you see Diego, I want to go along."

"Don't look so worried," Josephine said. Her eyes sparkled as she smiled at Martha. "I won't run away. Not with daddy so sick. Today was—just an impulse. I'd have come back. And besides, I've promised you."

The next day the weather changed. Martha woke to gray mist outside her window, and although it lifted as the morning passed, the overcast remained. Following lunch, Sarah trailed after Josephine and Martha, wanting them to play cards with her. Josephine fled to the tower with her books, and Sarah departed disconsolately. After a bit Martha climbed to the tower and asked Josephine if she'd like to take a walk.

Josephine eyed her over the top of the book.

"Why don't *you* go for a walk, Martha?" she asked. "I can feel your restlessness filling up the tower and it's making me edgy. I'll be right here when you get back." She grinned at Martha. "Take a chance—believe me."

Martha looked at Josephine, trying to assess her. Was this the same Josephine she'd met that first day? It seemed to her there'd been a change in the short time she'd known the girl. For the better? Or was the change in Martha, her?

Martha turned away to look out the window. Somehow she'd slipped out of the habit of thinking of Josephine as her patient. Josephine was immature and childlike in many ways, but mentally ill...? Martha shook her head. Suicide attempts? Even if they had been, that didn't mean insanity. And Jules's prediction of depression following the party hadn't been fulfilled.

And what if the suicide attempts had actually been murder attempts as Josephine insisted? Martha stared out into the gray day. Who? Only Jules would benefit by Josephine's death....

Suddenly she turned and started for the stairs. "I think I will take a short walk," she said. "I—I feel stifled."

Martha picked up a jacket from her room and went down to the main floor. Cathleen was passing through the foyer on her way to the library.

"I see you're still around," Cathleen said, stopping. "I hope you've enough sense to know you're not wanted."

"Jules wants a nurse here," Martha said, keeping her voice flat.

Cathleen raised an eyebrow. "Oh, we know what he *really* wants."

I won't give her the satisfaction of saying he intends to replace me, Martha thought. *Let him tell her.* "Excuse me, I'm going for a walk," she said.

"Leaving the patient?"

"Josephine prefers to read." Despite her efforts to the contrary, annoyance crept into Martha's voice. She started to walk past, but Cathleen caught her arm.

"You won't get Jules or the money," she hissed, her face close to Martha's, her fingers digging into her arm. "I can make it so unpleasant for you you'll be sorry you ever saw Black Tor."

A door closed softly, and they both jumped. Cathleen dropped Martha's arm and stepped back. No one appeared. Martha walked out the front door.

The wind was chilly, and she huddled into her jacket as she rounded the house toward the rose garden. A wry smile twisted her lips as she thought of Cathleen's threat. What could the woman do that would be any worse than letting everyone know that Martha was Marty Collier?

The roses at Black Tor were fragrant, and Martha walked between the beds, marveling at the shades of color, each rose lovelier than the last.

Johann had loved roses, hothouse flowers, and had filled the rooms with vases of them, refusing to throw them out until the petals had fallen and they drooped in death. Reds had been his favorite, the deep, almost-black reds. There'd been flowers across his body when she'd found him, rose petals as red as his blood.

What will happen here when I leave? she wondered. *Will Josephine be found like Johann? Will everyone say, "Poor girl, she tried to kill herself before, you know. . . ."*

Why? The money, Josephine said. Her father knew she needed protection and was afraid for her now that he neared death.

There must be someone I can talk to about this, Martha thought. *Someone I can trust.* But she trusted no one at Black Tor except Norman Garrard, and he was dying.

Dr. Marston? No. He himself had told her of generations of family ties with the Garrards. Anything she said to him would find its way back to Jules.

Bran? After all, it was his car that had been forced off the road. Had that been an accident? Or was it another attempt to get rid of Josephine? *We all might have died,* Martha thought. She shivered at the notion.

But she hesitated about Bran. *I'll try to see Miss Eccles at the hospital first,* she decided. *I'll ask her about Jose-*

phine's last so-called suicide attempt. Meanwhile, I must be careful. Very careful.

She heard voices and looked around for the source. Two men stood several yards away by the rhododendron bushes. Gardeners? Yes, one was Bill Wong. The other man raised his arm and Martha gasped, believing he was about to strike the gardener. But he didn't, turning instead and striding toward her. Then she realized it was Matthew.

For a second he seemed taken aback, but then walked up to her. "Insolent chap," he said, jerking his head toward the bushes where Bill now knelt in the dirt. "I've never been fond of Chinese servants."

Martha recalled the gardener's abrupt dismissal of her the one time she'd spoken to him. "He isn't very friendly," she said.

"I shouldn't allow myself to get so worked up," Matthew said. He smiled at Martha. "Where are you off to?"

"Nowhere. Just a walk."

"May I join you?"

She smiled at him, hoping her reluctance didn't show. Her last encounter with Matthew hadn't made her like his company.

"Have you noticed the topiary work at the end of the gardens?" he asked as they moved off together.

"Topiary? You mean those bushes pruned into different shapes? I remember seeing a swan and an elephant."

"You haven't noticed the totem?" He waved his hand toward where hedges marked the edge of the grass.

"A real totem pole?" she asked.

"No—it's actually an evergreen shrub, but very cleverly trained and pruned. Norman used to have a topiary specialist come in to do the clipping, and I believe Jules now does the same."

As he spoke he walked toward the hedge, and Martha followed. They came to the shrubs clipped into the shapes of animals, and she saw the inevitable killer whale, as well as a leaping salmon.

"Here's the totem," Matthew said. "Note the four animals surrounding it—bear, raven, eagle, wolf. The four Indian tribes of British Columbia. The Indians are a fascinating people, and it's a shame they weren't left alone to develop without our interference. I've no doubt they would have achieved a civilization superior to ours." Matthew's eyes glittered as he spoke—eyes as gray as the sky. "In my small way, I try to collect the evidence of the past. I keep the legends alive. Of course, with enough money I could...."

"Do you...." Martha hesitated, then began again. "Do you think it wise to tell Sarah those tales of monsters and woods demons? She's only six and doesn't understand the difference between fancy and fact. I have the feeling she believes in your Shishchuikul."

"Do you know he *doesn't* exist?" Matthew asked.

"Oh, please."

"What's your evidence for disbelief?" Matthew persisted.

"I don't think a little girl should be told those stories," Martha went on, ignoring his question. "Not as fact. She obviously likes and trusts you, so quite naturally she believes what you say."

"Didn't your husband believe in the existence of demons and warlocks? Didn't he believe in hell?" Matthew asked.

Martha recoiled as though he'd struck her.

Matthew smiled, his eyes metallic. "Hell exists—oh, yes, there's a hell. Don't you question my beliefs, young woman."

She stood staring at him for another few seconds, then turned and ran back to the house. She was breathless as she came into the sitting room.

Charn stood in her path.

I can't take another unpleasant encounter, she thought. "I must see about Josephine," she said, trying to go around him.

"Josephine will wait a few moments more," he said. "I saw you running away from Uncle Matthew. Did he make a pass at you?"

"No," she said coldly.

"Now I've made you angry again. We had such fun fishing that day. I thought you liked me."

"Please, Charn, I don't have time."

"Martha, I'm sorry. Don't keep looking at me with that cold Scot scorn. I—misjudged you. But I truly am attracted to you. Can't we be friends?" He smiled. "I'll behave. I'll be so platonic you won't believe it."

She hesitated, anxious to get away. "I'll think about it," she told him at last, then started around him again.

At the same time he threw out his arm to stop her, and it caught her in the side, throwing her off balance. He grabbed her, holding her steady, and she leaned against him for a second.

"I didn't hurt you, did I?" he asked. Still holding her, he peered into her face.

"I'm all right," she assured him, trying to pull away.

"I hope you don't think I did that on purpose," he said, keeping his hand firmly on her shoulder.

A flicker of movement caught Martha's eyes, and she turned her head to see Jules standing in the doorway. She shrugged away Charn's hand.

"I didn't mean to interrupt," Jules said.

"I..." Martha began, then stopped. She wouldn't explain. What was the difference? Jules thought she was a Nida, anyway. He wouldn't believe her.

CHAPTER EIGHTEEN

MARTHA PUSHED PAST both the men and hurried up to the tower. Josephine still sat on the floor, her back against a window seat, reading. She put the book down when Martha appeared.

"You weren't gone long," she said. "Did you have a nice walk?"

"I met Matthew," Martha told her. "I hadn't realized he was such a fanatic on Indian legends. We—upset each other."

"Oh, you can't argue with Uncle Matthew," Josephine said. "In his own way he's a match for Natalie. He's always fussing at Jules because there isn't more money for his great Indian projects." She stood up and stretched. "Why don't you find Sarah, and the three of us can play one of her card games? She was pouting because I wouldn't play crazy eights earlier."

"Up here?"

"No—let's go down to my bedroom. Sarah's either in her room or Louella's, maybe. Or else the classroom. You know where that is. Louella has a bedroom in daddy's wing. The first room to your right after you pass the stuffed raven."

Sarah wasn't in her room, although her deck of cards lay scattered on her bed. The classroom was empty.

Martha walked into the other wing and knocked on Louella's door. There was no response. After a moment she knocked again, and was about to turn away, when the door eased open and Louella peered out at her.

"Is Sarah with you?" Martha asked.

"Oh, no. No."

"Do you know where she might be?"

"I don't."

"Well, thank you." Martha had begun to turn away, when Louella fastened thin fingers on her arm.

"Come in. I have something to say to you." Louella's voice was so low that Martha had to lean close to hear her. She went into the room and Louella closed the door behind her.

Martha sat in a lyre-backed chair with a plum velvet seat, while Louella sat across from her in an antique oak platform rocker. A child's spool rocker sat empty beside Louella.

"Sarah likes you," Louella said.

"I like her, too," Martha answered. "She's a—remarkable child."

"She extremely intelligent and very sensible. Those two qualities are not often associated."

Martha looked at the old woman, who sat quietly in her neat navy dress, hands folded in her lap. "I do think, though, that she ought to have friends her age to play with—at least occasionally," Martha said.

"I quite agree. One of the gardeners brought his grandson several times, but unfortunately Natalie didn't approve. She can be snobbish—as if all that matters to a child. Jimmy Smithson is a bright boy, a good companion for Sarah at this age."

Louella was responsible for getting Bill Wong's grandson to play with Sarah? Martha gazed at her with more respect.

"I hope to find another playmate for Sarah soon," the

old woman said. "As you've mentioned, it *is* important. You're a sensible person yourself, as I've noted."

This was intended as a compliment, Martha knew. She smiled.

"So I've decided to tell you about Clara Eccles. There was a cord tied across the steps, near the top. She tripped over the cord and fell. I saw the cord myself, but we all dithered around after the accident, and when I went back up the stairs the cord was gone. I meant to tell Jules— Norman was too ill by then—but when I couldn't find a trace of what I'd seen, I said nothing." She tightened her lips. "One of the curses of aging is that young people tend to treat you as senile."

"So Miss Eccles was right when she said her fall was no accident?"

"Yes. I've visited her at St. Joseph's since the accident and she told me someone knocked on her door and when she opened it no one was there. But then someone called her name from downstairs, so she came to see who, and that's when she fell."

"Miss Eccles doesn't know about the cord?"

"You're the first person I've told, besides her," Louella said. "Clara Eccles is safe enough at St. Joseph's. You, however, are at Black Tor and are not safe. Sarah tells me everything that goes on in the house, and she misses very little. I've heard about the picnic near the cliff. I've also heard of the car in which you were riding being forced off the road yesterday."

"Josephine's the one who's not safe," Martha said.

"I realize that. But she belongs here at Black Tor. You don't. You have the freedom to leave. I'm powerless to help either of you, except by warning you to leave."

"But couldn't you tell Jules about the cord now?" Martha asked.

"No. I imagine you've heard how his wife, Cynthia, fell

on those same stairs. He's brooded about her accident for years. He doesn't want any reminders of Clara Eccles's similar fall and would dismiss my story about a cord as being senile. I'll be quite frank. I have no money, no income of any kind. Norman, through Jules, supports me. Norman is dying. I don't mean to insinuate that Jules begrudges me a place in the house. But if I were too much of a burden, I feel I might be sent to a home for old people. I couldn't bear such a life. I am careful never to—intrude."

"Does Jules handle all the money? I mean—his father is still alive. . . ."

"Norman still signs the checks. He'll give up his hold on the money only in death. But he *is* dying. Jules makes the decisions." Louella rose from her chair. "Don't count on Jules, my dear, for I don't believe he'll marry again."

Martha rose, too, and stood facing the old woman. "Is Sarah Jules's child?" she asked.

"I've never been sure. Abel Garrard was a great womanizer, and he took years to remarry after Norman's mother died. Norman has two bastard half brothers in Victoria that I know of. There may have been others. It's possible that Sarah could be a grandchild of those men—the Garrard strain is very strong."

"But why would Jules take her in?"

"He didn't. Norman did. That's why I've wondered."

Martha walked to the door. "Thank you for asking me in," she said. "I see you're concerned for Sarah, and I'm glad to know someone is. I—I won't be at Black Tor much longer. Jules is looking now for my replacement."

"I'm sure the decision is best for you," Louella said. "Goodbye, my dear." She closed the door.

Martha stood in the hall, frozen in position with the sudden thought that maybe a cord had been tied across the stairs twice, once for Cynthia, then for Clara Eccles. Then she shook her head and started down the hall. Why would anyone want to kill Jules's wife? She was growing paranoid.

But someone did want Josephine dead. Didn't Louella care at all? She seemed to know that Josephine was in danger. How could she do nothing?

What am I doing? Martha asked herself. *Should I go to the police?* Yet what proof did she have? They certainly wouldn't even listen to the story of an American nurse, a nobody, with an unfounded tale about one of the wealthiest families in Victoria.

"Martha!" Sarah's voice.

She whirled around.

"Martha—oh, Martha...."

The child ran toward her from the wing Martha had just left. When she reached her, Sarah clung to her, burying her face in Martha's side. "He's dead, not asleep at all—I touched him and he was cold. Oh, Martha...."

Norman has died and Sarah found him, Martha thought. *The poor child.* "I'll go and look, Sarah. Let me go. I'll take you to Louella's room. Where's Simon? Did you see him?"

"But—but that's who—it's Simon. He's dead...."

"Simon!"

Martha detached Sarah and took her to Louella, then hurried to Norman Garrard's quarters. Simon was sprawled on his face in the doorway between the inner and outer rooms. She knelt beside him, but knew as she felt for a pulse that Sarah had reported accurately. Simon was cold. And dead.

Martha rose and went to Norman's bedside. His face was bluish. For a moment she thought that he, too, had died, but then she found the faint flicker of a pulse in his wrist. She missed something in the room, looked about her and realized that the oxygen wasn't bubbling in the water bottle attached to the tank. She checked the gauge; the tank was empty.

She pushed the intercom button to alert Francis downstairs and then brought the spare oxygen tank from the corner by the closet. A wrench on a chain hung over the cap. She switched gauges and attached the bottle to the new tank. Soon oxygen flowed into Norman's lungs once again, and the mottled blueness of his face began to pink up.

Martha heard a sound and saw Francis standing short of the doorway on the other side of Simon's body, eyes wide and shocked. He looked from her to the body and back.

"Call the doctor! Get Jules! Hurry!" she commanded.

Martha checked over the array of medications on the dresser but was afraid to administer any of them until the doctor came. She watched Norman's face, her hand on his wrist.

"Good God!" Jules stepped over Simon's body and came to the side of the bed. "Is he. . .?"

"Your father's unconscious, but alive. Did Francis call the doctor?"

"Yes. He'll be out immediately."

"He—your father—should be in a hospital."

"No. I've promised him I would keep him at home." He turned his head to look at the door. "Simon?"

"Dead. I don't know why. After I found him I came in here to see if your father was all right, and the oxygen tank was empty and I had to change it and I—didn't look at Simon again."

"Why were you in here?" Jules asked.

"Sarah found Simon and called me," Martha said.

"Sarah!"

"She used to visit your father. I sent her in to Louella."

Norman's eyelids fluttered.

Martha lowered her voice. "He may hear us." She moved away from the bed and Jules followed her.

"Is there anything we can do for—him?" Jules said softly. He jerked his head toward Simon.

"No. I don't want to move him until the doctor gets here and has a look at him."

"You don't think he died naturally?" Jules asked.

"I don't know. Simon wouldn't let the oxygen tank go empty. Was he trying to come in and change it when he...?"

"...matter with you, Francis, I—" The unmistakable voice of Natalie sounded from the hall.

Jules hurried through the outer room and stopped her at the door. "You aren't to come in now, Aunt Natalie," he said.

"I must see Norman," she said.

"He's all right. Simon's dead. You can't come in here until the doctor's had a look at Simon."

"Simon!"

"Please, Natalie...."

"I don't understand."

"Neither do we. I'll tell you what I can later." He shut the door before she could protest further and returned to Martha.

"Jules," she said, "something's terribly wrong at Black Tor. I think the doctor will find that Simon didn't die naturally, that he was murdered. I don't know why someone wanted to kill him, but it must be part of the other—Josephine's nearly dying three times and *not* of her own doing, Miss Eccles tripping over a cord and falling on the stairs and me being drugged at the cliffside. Then yesterday...."

"What's this about a cord and Miss Eccles?"

"Louella told me," Martha said. "She's afraid you wouldn't believe her and might turn her out. But she saw a cord the night Miss Eccles fell. Then someone removed it before she could tell you."

Jules appeared stunned.

Is he thinking of Cynthia's fall? Martha wondered.

"Louella should have told me," he said at last. "What were you saying about yesterday?"

"Bran's car was nearly sideswiped by a truck. Fortunately his brakes are good and he was able to stop, so we didn't have an accident. But I can't help thinking we were meant to. Josephine, Sarah and me. And Bran, of course, though I don't think anyone's after him. Perhaps not Sarah, either." She shuddered. "I can't imagine the mind of anyone who would involve the other three of us just to do away with Josephine."

Jules put his arm around her. "It could have been just a random accident—trucks do run cars off the road, after all."

Martha shook her head and gave way to the impulse to lean against Jules. His arms tightened, she felt his mouth on her temple, and she longed to turn her face up to him, to hold him. . . .

Instead she pulled away and went to Norman's bedside. His pulse was stronger and his color improved.

"How is he?" Jules said in a half whisper.

"Holding his own."

"You won't be able to leave as soon as I had planned." Jules frowned. "I'll need to find someone to care for my father, another nurse. Would you take care of him until I do? You'll have to sleep in here, I'm afraid."

"Of course I'll stay with him," she said. "He does need full-time nursing. You really ought to have more than one nurse—for relief, you know. And he—your father—prefers women."

Jules smiled. "Yes, I know he does. I'll make sure he has his preference." The smile faded. "For the time he has left," he said.

There was a knock at the door.

"That must be Will," Jules said. "Dr. Hansen."

But it was Francis. Martha watched Jules talk to him at the outer door, and when he came back to her his face was grim.

"The doctor was delayed," he said. "There's been an accident on the grounds. Henry had just run up to the house to call for help when the doctor drove up. He's attending to Bill now."

"Bill Wong?"

"Yes."

"What happened?"

"Francis said Bill was shot."

CHAPTER NINETEEN

THE DOCTOR WAS a tall sandy-haired man, and as Martha watched his competent examination of Norman Garrard, she wondered if he'd been summoned to Black Tor for the other accidents—Cynthia, Clara Eccles. Should she talk to him about what was going on? Jules had called him by his first name—were they close friends?

Norman was semiconscious, rousing when someone moved him, but he couldn't speak. Dr. Hansen turned from the bed at last and knelt beside Simon's body. "Have you called the police?" he asked. "I must report your gardener's gunshot wound, you know."

"Yes," Jules told him. "They're on the way."

Dr. Hansen rose. "I wouldn't be able to determine a cause of death here without an autopsy, since I've never attended this young man. Do you know if he saw a doctor recently?"

Jules shook his head. "I don't have any idea."

The three of them regarded Simon's motionless body.

"Best to leave him as he is, since the police are coming," Dr. Hansen said. He turned back to Norman's bed and looked at Martha. "You're a registered nurse?" he asked.

"Yes."

Dr. Hansen motioned Martha and Jules toward a window, where he spoke in low tones. "There's to be no heroics, Miss—" He paused.

"Jamison," Martha said after glancing at Jules. "Martha Jamison."

Dr. Hansen gave a quick nod. "I've promised your father, as you know, Jules. No hospital, no heroics." The doctor spoke in a half whisper. "He *is* dying. A matter of hours or days—but soon. We'll try to keep him comfortable. You do understand, Miss Jamison?"

She nodded. "I understand."

Dr. Hansen's eyes held hers, and he looked at her closely for several moments. "Very good," he said at last. "I'll come anytime you call me. Although...." He shrugged, then added, "There's really nothing more I can do for Norman except leave him in peace. I'll speak to the police about the need for a decent amount of haste in getting their business finished so we won't disturb him any more than necessary." He stepped over Simon's body and strode to the outer door. Jules followed.

Martha hesitated, then went back to the bedside. Norman's eyes were closed, and although his lips were fairly pink, a pallor circled his mouth. She looked at his fingernails and saw the bluish tinge that meant his damaged heart was unable to pump enough oxygen to the tissues, despite the extra oxygen flowing into his lungs from the green cylinder.

As she touched his wrist to check his pulse, he opened his eyes. His lips formed a word, though no sound came from them. "Simon."

"I'm taking care of you now, Mr. Garrard," Martha said, keeping her voice calm and clear. "Simon is—ill."

To her alarm, Norman struggled to raise his head so that he could see the rest of the room. She urged him back against the pillows.

"Rest," she told him. "Don't exert yourself."

"Dead," gasped Norman. "I know." He stared into her eyes and she saw that his pupils were dilated. "Have to...." Once again he strove to raise himself. "I know who..." he said quite clearly as he levered himself and turned toward the door.

He can see Simon's body! she thought. Norman's face mottled with the effort, and she grasped at his wrist. "Please lie back," she said. "There's nothing you can do for Simon. Dr. Hansen—"

"Dead," Norman repeated, and fell back onto the pillows.

Under her fingers his pulse flickered and faded. His mouth opened and she heard his breathing change.

"Doctor!" she called. But Dr. Hansen had gone with Jules.

Norman was dying. Not in hours or days, but that moment. His pulse was almost gone, his breathing was shallower and the rales in his chest were ever more obvious—the rattle of dying lungs.

Martha had schooled herself not to fear death, and she knew she could do nothing more for Norman Garrard. If she went for the doctor, Norman would be dead when she returned. Still, her neck prickled with apprehension. Simon's body lay between her and the outside door, and now Norman's breathing had stopped. She felt trapped inside the death-filled room.

A stethoscope lay on the nightstand, and she fitted the earpieces in, then bent over to listen to Norman's chest. There was no sound. She removed the stethoscope and shut off the oxygen.

I mustn't let this effect me, she told herself. *I've been away from nursing too long, that's what's wrong.* But she glanced around her with terror, as though death might be visible after all.

Johann had been lying in his own blood when she'd found him, but his skin was still warm. If she'd come out a few seconds earlier, could she have saved him? She made a sound of protest and the small noise in the silent room startled her into awareness.

I must find Dr. Hansen, she thought. *And Jules.*

But as she stepped over Simon's body, the outer door opened and Jules was there with two strange men, one in uniform.

The police.

Martha hurried to Jules. "Your father just died," she said. "Where's Dr. Hansen?"

Jules stood for a moment without speaking.

"Your father, sir?" one of the men said.

"The doctor's in the library," Jules said to Martha. "With Bill Wong. Waiting for the ambulance." He glanced toward Norman's bed and back at Martha. "I can't quite...."

"I'll get Dr. Hansen," Martha said, moving past the three men and hurrying down the corridor toward the stairs. Before she started down, she saw a stretcher with a blanketed figure being pushed across the foyer toward the front door by two attendants. Dr. Hansen followed behind, but he stopped when she called to him. She met him halfway down the stairs and explained what had happened.

Later, when the hearse had come and gone, Martha went in search of Josephine and found her in the tower.

"The black remover's van," Josephine said to her.

Martha stared at her.

"Don't you read Auden?" Josephine asked. "That's from one of his poems." Tears glittered in her eyes.

"Josephine...."

"I didn't love him, I didn't!" Josephine voice rose. "Why do I feel so bad?"

Martha sat next to her on the window seat and put an arm around her. "Your father was an old man," she said. "He was sick and uncomfortable...."

Josephine turned away and put her hands over her face.

"I know," she said. "But he didn't want to die—no one wants to die!"

This from a girl who'd supposedly tried to kill herself more than once? Martha shook her head. She no longer believed that Josephine had ever tried suicide.

Josephine turned back to her. "He never loved me," she said. "Or my mother, either."

"I think you're wrong," Martha told her. "I don't know how he felt about your mother, but every time I talked to him, his one concern was for your safety."

"Only because I'm a part of him—his daughter. Not because I'm me." Tears rolled down Josephine's face. "He just loved Jules. Jules is *her* son. The first Josephine. Josie."

"Didn't you tell me your father left everything equally to you and Jules?"

"I didn't say he wasn't fair." Josephine began to sob, and her words came through with difficulty. "Only he never loved me...."

Martha held her while she cried, feeling tears gather in her own eyes.

At last Josephine straightened herself, wiping her face with a handkerchief, reducing it to a sodden ball. "Poor Simon," she said when she'd finished. "They took him away, too, didn't they? I never liked Simon, but I didn't wish him dead."

"Then you know?" Martha asked.

"Sarah told me."

Martha started up. "I left her with Louella. Where—"

"Don't go," Josephine begged. "Sarah's all right. I was down in my room when she came in. Then Aunt Nat collected her." She dabbed the last of the tears from her eyes. "What happened to Simon? I saw the police. Were they here about Bill, or was Simon...?" She stopped, looking at Martha.

"Dr. Hansen doesn't know what killed Simon. He—it might have been a natural death. The police checked because—well, there could've been an accident."

"Or someone could have killed him, too, isn't that right?"

"Too?" Martha asked.

"Like they tried to do with me. And you. Accidents."

"I don't know," Martha told her.

"And Bill Wong was shot," Josephine added. "Another accident?"

"I—assumed it had been," Martha said. "The woods. . . ."

"Our land is all posted," Josephine said. "No one hunts here."

"Still. . . ."

"I don't believe it," Josephine said.

Martha agreed with her but thought it best not to say so. "Let's go down to our bedrooms," she said to Josephine. "I realize you don't feel like eating, but. . . ."

"It'll be just like Jules to insist we all appear for dinner as usual," Josephine said bitterly. "And I suppose I'll have to. Jules will be watching me, waiting for me to act peculiar so he can put me in one of those places and get control of my money." Her mouth tightened and her face grew tense. In that moment Martha thought Josephine looked a good deal like her half brother.

Josephine caught at Martha's arm. "You won't have to leave Black Tor now!" she cried. "I can pay you to stay—to be my companion! You'll stay, won't you?"

"I'll stay if you want me," Martha said. "But there's Diego, too."

Josephine shook her head. "We have to wait," she said. "I don't want Jules to know about Diego. Not until the money's in my name."

"You promised me I could meet Diego," Martha reminded her.

Josephine eyed her warily. "He says not yet."

Martha looked away, her mind filled with mistrust of the reluctant Diego, missing all these years and now returning just as Josephine came into a fortune.

"I'll be twenty-three in a week," Josephine said. "Daddy thought he'd live past my birthday. He knew I wasn't crazy. That's why he changed his will last year. Before that, Jules was my guardian and had control of my share of the money if daddy died. But last year the will was changed so that I had control of my own money when I reached twenty-three. So I won't get my share until next week, when I have my birthday. And I suppose there'll be delays, so I won't really have it for months after. But I'll pay you when I can, Martha."

"Don't worry about paying me," Martha said. "I'll stay as long as you need me."

As she followed Josephine down the winding stairs from the tower, Martha wondered how she could protect Josephine as Norman had asked. From whom? Diego? Jules? Someone else at Black Tor? Charn? Cathleen? Natalie? Or Matthew? Could Louella be a threat to anyone? Martha didn't trust any of them.

In her bedroom Martha changed into a cotton print skirt—not especially appropriate for a Black Tor dinner, but it would have to do.

Josephine came in looking pale and subdued in a navy dress with white piping around the collar. She knocked against the stand that held the gilt cage with the stuffed canary, and the yellow bird swung dumbly on its perch. They both watched the tiny swing go to and fro. Martha's mouth twisted in distaste.

"I don't like them, either," Josephine said, turning her face from the cage. "I'm sorry I threw the cat from the tower and frightened you when you first came, but I'm glad I got rid of one more dead pet. I—it's morbid, all different kinds of animals in the house and none of them alive. But daddy wouldn't let anything be different from the way his father did it.'' She swung around and glared at the stuffed canary. ''And Jules won't change things, either. I'm glad daddy left him the house. I don't want it.''

They met Louella in the hall by the staircase.

''How is Sarah?'' she asked.

''Aunt Nat took her somewhere,'' Josephine said. ''But she didn't seem upset when I talked to her. Excited, perhaps.''

Louella shook her head. ''I trust Natalie put Sarah to bed,'' she said. ''The child's too young to encounter so much death. Finding the young man—and then she loved Norman.''

Josephine glanced sharply at Louella, but the old woman started to pick her way down the stairs, moving slowly and carefully. *I wonder if she checks each time for a cord?* Martha thought suddenly. *Does she think someone wishes her ill?*

''That's the ugliest one of all,'' Josephine said. ''But Jules won't ever part with her.''

''With what?''

Josephine gestured at the killer whale rising from the foyer toward them. ''She belongs in a museum. I used to be afraid of the whale when I was little, and then when I found out she was a girl I stopped being scared, but I've never....''

Josephine paused, her foot arrested in the air. ''What's that?'' she demanded, pointing.

Martha saw what she meant: a white object—was it paper?—on the orca's tail.

''The writing's in green!'' Josephine cried. ''My name!'' She rushed down the rest of the steps, pushing past Louella, with Martha following close behind.

Josephine ran to the whale and reached up for the paper.

"Diego must have written me!" she said. Then she stood on her toes to yank at the paper, pulling impatiently against the tape holding it to the orca's tail. Martha, behind her, heard Louella cry out.

"Oh, dear God—it's going to fall!"

Martha saw the pedestal buckle as Josephine jerked at the envelope, and she screamed and lunged at Josephine, grabbing her, trying to pull her sideways. And then there was a grinding noise, and something hit her across the chest and flung her to the floor. After that, nothing....

CHAPTER TWENTY

VOICES IN THE DARKNESS, hands touching her, a man calling her name. Martha opened her eyes with an effort, surprised to find herself lying on the floor.

"Are you all right, Martha?" Jules's voice.

She looked up into his eyes. "I—think so." She moved her legs tentatively, then her arms, and winced with pain. "My shoulder...."

She turned her head and saw the broken body of the killer whale littering the foyer floor. Someone had said the whale was falling; someone had screamed....

Josephine!

Martha struggled to a sitting position, ignoring the pain in her left shoulder. She tried to rise to her feet, but a wave of dizziness prevented her. "Josephine?" she asked. "Is she...?"

"She's alive." Jules's voice was grim.

Martha looked frantically about and saw Josephine lying in back of her. Holding her left arm across her body, Martha slid herself over next to the unconscious girl.

Josephine's pulse was weak but steady.

"Have you called Dr. Hansen, an ambulance?" Martha asked.

Jules crouched on the other side of Josephine. "The ambulance should be here any moment. Will Hansen's already at St. Joseph's and will meet the ambulance there." He touched Josephine's face awkwardly, pushing back a strand of hair.

"Can you tell how badly hurt she is?" he asked.

Martha shook her head. "Don't move her," she said.

"What happened?" someone asked.

Martha glanced up and saw Natalie. Matthew stood beside her. Charn was in the foyer, too, and Cathleen. Francis hovered near the shattered bulk of the orca, as though waiting for orders to clean up the mess.

Suddenly everyone began to speak.

"I heard Louella call out," Cathleen said. "Then a scream...."

"And the thud—I knew what had happened before I ran in," Charn said.

"I can't imagine how the whale came to fall," Matthew said. "Were you fooling with the pedestal?"

"A note," Martha said. "There was an envelope taped to the tail with Josephine's name written in green. She...." Her words trailed off. No point in mentioning Diego.

"Are you saying Josephine pulled the whale over on the two of you?" Natalie asked. "Impossible."

"It fell," Martha said. "Louella called out to warn us, but I couldn't get Josephine out of the way."

The note. Had Josephine pulled it free of the tail? Was it under the debris now?

"Who was the letter from?" Jules asked, as if reading her mind.

"I—don't know. Josephine might not even have been able to free the envelope before...."

"An odd place to put a message," Matthew said.

Martha stared down at Josephine's white face. The pulse remained steady under her fingers, but the girl showed no signs of regaining consciousness.

"The whale shouldn't have fallen," Jules stated. "The fastenings are checked every month or so."

"Exactly what I said," Natalie put in. "That's what we

get for taking an adventuress into the house. I warned you, Jules. I said a young woman with her looks was up to no good applying for a job like this. I told you—"

"Aunt Natalie," Jules said, "please be quiet. Martha is in no way responsible for this accident."

"That museum fellow," Charn said. "The one you said was interested in the whale. Could he have done something?"

Bran? Martha thought. Surely he had nothing to do with this. And yet he *had* been fascinated by the killer whale. Could he have inadvertently loosened a fastening?

"I doubt it was Lowrey," Jules said. He glanced at Martha, then at Josephine.

At that moment the ambulance arrived, and Martha rode to the hospital with Josephine.

At St. Joseph's, an X ray revealed that Martha's collarbone was broken, and after a wait Dr. Hansen put her arm in a sling.

"Have you found how badly Josephine's injured?" Martha asked him. "Is she conscious?"

"No skull fracture, though I suspect a concussion. She's responding quite well. Fracture of the fourth and fifth ribs, right side, but the lung's not involved. A few days here in the hospital should have her feeling well enough to go home. As for you...." Dr. Hansen paused and looked at her for a long moment. "I can keep you here overnight if you like. You've a few bruises besides the fractured clavicle."

"But I don't really need to stay at the hospital," Martha said.

"No." He still watched her. "Not unless you want to."

She looked back at him uncertainly.

"An odd accident after the whale sat there all these years," Dr. Hansen said. "Will you be staying long at Black Tor?"

Did he suspect she was responsible? Or was he warning her? But of what?

"I'll stay until Josephine no longer needs me," she said. "May I see her?"

"Yes, of course. For a few minutes. I've assigned a nurse to her for tonight—you won't be allowed to remain in her room. Come back and visit her tomorrow by all means."

Jules drove Martha back to the house. They rode through the night in silence until he turned the car into the private road leading to Black Tor.

"I'm glad your injury isn't too serious," he said. "I want you to stay until you feel well enough to travel. This has been...." He hesitated. "I'm sorry about—everything," he went on. "I wish...." Again he stopped, and this time he said nothing more.

What shall I tell him? Martha wondered. *That I won't go if Josephine needs me? And what does he wish? That I had never been Marty Collier? I wish it, too. But I was, I am, and the fact can't be changed.* She was very conscious of Jules next to her in the small car, wanting him to touch her and yet afraid he would.

"You should be safe," Jules said. "With Josephine in the hospital...."

"Safe?"

"Stay in your room except for meals. Tedious, I know, but...."

"Then you believe me about the accidents—you realize someone's trying to kill Josephine! You—"

"Martha, don't put words in my mouth. I don't want anything more to happen to you. Let's leave it at that."

"But Josephine—"

"She's certainly safe at St. Joseph's Hospital."

"Yes, but—"

"I plan to have my father's safety-deposit box opened as

soon as possible,'' Jules said. "He hid things from me—he always has. I've given up trying to understand why. This mystery about Josephine, for example. The years she was gone. He must know—he brought her back. And yet he would tell no one, not even Louis Marston."

"Or Dr. Hansen?'' Martha asked. "Hasn't he ever taken care of Josephine before? Dr. Marston's a psychiatrist."

Jules sighed. "I know. But Louis has been Josephine's only doctor. When she took the pills those two times, he came to the house and treated her there."

"That's—unusual," Martha said.

"And when she fell over the cliff, my father wouldn't let him keep her at the hospital. When the X rays showed no fractures, he insisted she come home."

"I wonder why," Martha said.

"And there's Sarah. Father told me nothing of her origins. Obviously she's an illegitimate Garrard."

Martha said nothing.

"No, she's not my child!" Jules spoke vehemently. "I know half the town believes she is, and I've often felt my father chose to have them think so. God knows why."

"There's been some suggestion that your grandfather Abel had illegitimate children," Martha said tentatively.

Jules sighed again. "Yes. But why wouldn't my father let me know that that was where Sarah's Garrard blood came from? And why bring her to Black Tor to begin with? He was never interested himself in his father's byblows or their descendents before."

The lights of the house were before them, and Jules pulled up by the front door. Martha had a sudden reluctance to get out of the car and go into the house. She turned toward Jules. He leaned over and touched her face, then kissed her gently.

After a moment she pulled away, afraid to prolong the

embrace. He hesitated, then got out and came around to open her door. "I'll send Ruth to your room," he told her. "You'll have trouble managing with your arm in that sling."

"Thank you."

He opened the front door.

Charn stood in the foyer, his face tense, all the laugh lines gone. "I'm glad you're back, Jules," he said. "Sarah's disappeared."

"What do you mean, 'disappeared'?"

Charn shrugged. "We can't find Sarah. Cousin Louella started nattering away about the kid right after you left, and at first none of us paid any attention. Then—"

"Oh, thank heaven you're here, Jules!" said Natalie, coming out of the library and crossing to the foyer where they stood. "Little Sarah is gone. We can't find her anywhere."

"You've searched the house?" Jules asked. "The tower, too?"

"Cathleen went up there herself," Natalie said. "Francis, Ruth, Henry—we've all been looking. Sarah's not in the house. Henry even went outside and called her, but with no results."

"Who saw her last?" Jules demanded. "And when?"

"Louella claims I took her," Natalie said. "What actually happened was Sarah ran off from Louella and she won't admit it. I found the child in Josephine's room...." Natalie paused and shook her head. "I don't seem able to absorb all that's happened today. Simon's death and then Norman...." She dabbed at her eyes with a lace-edged handkerchief.

"Where did you take Sarah?" Jules asked.

"To her own room, of course. I felt she needed to rest away from the excitement—the ambulance and the police. She gets very worked up."

"Then what?"

"Why, I left her in her room, with instructions to rest on her bed with the door closed until dinner."

"You didn't go back and check on her?" Martha asked.

Natalie shot her a venomous glance. "With all the commotion, I had no chance to see Sarah again until Louella asked about her." Natalie spoke directly to Jules, ignoring Martha as much as she could.

"When did you realize Sarah was gone?" Jules said.

"Louella insisted she wasn't in her room, so I went with Louella to look—this was after the ambulance had left. The child wasn't there. Louella became positively hysterical, demanding we find Sarah immediately. I confess I wasn't worried at the time. You know what a gamine Sarah is, constantly evading rules...."

Cathleen came down the staircase. "I rechecked all the bedrooms in the south wing," she said. "I even looked inside the storage space under the windows seats in the tower."

Jules shut his eyes briefly and took a deep breath. "I'll notify the police," he said.

"Oh, Jules, do you think that wise?" Natalie asked. "Sarah could just be hiding somewhere."

"She's only six years old," Jules said. "It's almost midnight." He strode into the library.

Martha hurried after him. Sarah had been left in her own bedroom that afternoon after Natalie had brought her from Josephine's room. Why hadn't she sought out Josephine again—in the tower? She trusted Josephine. Wait—maybe she had. Perhaps Josephine had been the last to see her....

Jules was talking on the phone as Martha came into the library. She waited until he had finished.

"Josephine might have seen Sarah," she said. "Josephine was in the tower until just before the accident.

Maybe Sarah went up there and talked to her.''

Jules listened, his face closed and harsh. "That's merely conjecture. We'll ask Josephine, of course, but I don't count on anything." He rubbed his face. "Do you think the child could have gone outside?"

"I just don't know, Jules. Sarah isn't a fearful girl. She might have."

"Would she have spoken to strangers? Gotten into a car?"

"Wouldn't any strange car here at Black Tor have been remarked on?"

"At night? Look here—you don't think your friend Lowrey actually did engineer that accident with the whale and then waylay Sarah, do you?"

"Bran?" Martha was incredulous.

"Well, Sarah knew him. She'd have gone off with him, wouldn't she?"

"Yes, but I don't believe that Bran—oh, Jules, that's ridiculous."

"What do you actually know of the man?"

"I told you—I met him on the ferry from Seattle."

"Yes, that's what you've said."

"It's the truth!"

"Then he could have Sarah, for all you know."

She glared at Jules. "I don't know Bran well, but I can't believe he'd kidnap a child! He's not a—a child molester!"

"How can you be sure?"

"I've met a few in my psychiatric training," Martha snapped. "Bran doesn't fit the profile."

"Why are you protecting him?"

"I'm not. But you have no evidence—only your own dislike...."

"You're in love with him."

"No!" Martha's voice rose. "What's the matter with you, Jules?" She wanted to shake him, to scream at him that if she was in love with anyone it was with him, Jules Garrard.

Jules sat in the chair behind the desk and put his head in his hands.

Martha waited, but he said nothing more. She resisted the impulse to go to him and smooth his hair, cradle his head against her.

"You'd better get some rest," he said at last. "You've had a bad day."

"How can I rest with Sarah missing?"

"I'll take you to your room," he said. "You can't do anything tonight. Tomorrow we'll go to the hospital and talk to Josephine. In the meantime, you must get some sleep."

"But I—"

"Damn it!" he shouted. "Must you always argue with me?"

CHAPTER TWENTY-ONE

MARTHA HAD TAKEN two of the pain pills Dr. Hansen had given her for the fractured collarbone; otherwise she was sure she wouldn't have been able to sleep at all.

In the morning, after Jules had phoned the hospital to check on Josephine's condition, he asked Henry to take Martha to St. Joseph's.

"I thought you were coming, too," Martha said.

"I have to stop by the police station with photographs of Sarah," he said. "Then I have an appointment at the bank."

Wasn't he even going to visit Josephine? Martha wondered. And how could he be so calm about the missing Sarah? Did he have no feelings at all? Was he so unruffled by his father's death, the missing child and his sister's near-fatal accident that he'd slept through the night and now was going about his ordinary business?

Jules strode past her and in a moment she heard the roar of the MG going down the drive.

"We're all upset about Sarah, miss," Henry said as he handed Martha into the silver Rolls-Royce. "I hope they find her soon—I wouldn't want to think she was somewhere hurt or frightened. And Miss Josephine in the hospital...." He shook his head. "Even you, miss."

Yes, even me, Martha thought, adjusting the sling on her arm as she settled herself in the seat.

After a moment she was struck by the fact that she was the only one from the house going to the hospital to visit Josephine.

"And that Bill Wong," Henry went on. "I warned him he should mind his own business."

"What do you mean?" Martha asked.

"Well, you must realize Mrs. Garrard hired him. The second Mrs. Garrard, who was Miss Josephine's mother." Henry frowned. "I never met the lady, but she was well liked in the household. Felt sorry for her, they did, or so I've been told."

"What does she have to do with Bill Wong getting shot?"

"Well, he wanted to help Miss Josephine on account of her mother. That's why he took the letters from that man, whoever *he* was, and then the little girl delivered them."

"Sarah?" Martha remembered the first note Josephine had gotten from Diego. Bill Wong had given the note to Sarah to take to Josephine. "Do you think whoever shot Bill Wong has taken Sarah? But why?"

"Because, miss, it could be that she's seen him, whoever he is. She's a curious little girl, and it isn't like a proper watch is kept over her—begging your pardon, miss, but of course that's not your job."

"Do you know who this man is—the one Bill Wong took the letters from?"

Henry shook his head. "Never saw him close up, and Bill wasn't a talker. All I saw was someone give something to Bill two different times. But I wasn't near enough to recognize anyone. I watched to see what Bill did, and when he slipped a letter to little Sarah, I followed her to see what she did with it." He glanced sideways at Martha. "Likely you know about the letters."

Martha didn't answer. Could Diego be responsible for Sarah's disappearance after all? Had he shot Bill Wong? For what reason?

"Have you told Jules—Mr. Garrard?" she asked.

Henry shook his head. "Not yet. I've been thinking it through, like."

"You ought to talk to the police about what you've told me," Martha said. "Is Bill Wong too badly hurt to tell them anything?"

"I heard he was in the intensive care unit," Henry said. "Lost a lot of blood."

"Just drop me off at the hospital and then go and talk to the police," Martha said. "Maybe what you know will help them find Sarah."

"I'll do just that, if you think it might help," Henry said. "Mr. Jules told me to wait for you, but I suppose he'd want me to tell what I know...."

"You can come back for me when you've finished," Martha said.

At St. Joseph's, she hurried down the corridors, looking for Josephine's room, still feeling unbalanced by the sling. She must insist that Josephine tell her how to get in touch with Diego. Surely if she explained about Sarah.... The report Jules had gotten in the morning was that Josephine was sitting up and wanting to get dressed. If she felt that well, Martha need have no hesitation about forcing information from her.

But Josephine had a visitor. Martha stopped in the doorway in surprise when she saw Bran Lowrey sitting on the hospital bed. He rose hurriedly. Had he been holding Josephine's hand?

"Bran!" Martha exclaimed.

"I heard about the accident," he said. "Friends in high places." He grinned at her and once again the teasing sense of familiarity came over her. Something about his smile....

Josephine was sitting up, her cheeks were pink and she looked healthy and happy.

"Broken ribs," Bran said. "Plus banging her head. How could such an unlikely accident have happened?"

I *happen to have a broken clavicle,* Martha thought. *A lot you seem to care about that.*

"Someone wanted her hurt—or worse," Bran went on. "She can't go back there."

Martha stared at him in amazement. When she glanced at Josephine, she saw her gazing up at Bran with parted lips, her yellow eyes wide. Was Josephine interested in him? What about her long-lost love, Diego?

"I won't have it," Bran continued. "Martha, you can find an apartment for Jo and stay with her there. Don't worry about the damn money. I'll pay for it."

So Bran had already discovered that Josephine was an heiress. Perhaps that accounted for his sudden interest. Martha felt oddly disappointed in him.

"Sarah's missing," she said abruptly.

Josephine swung her head toward Martha. "Missing? What do you mean?"

"We can't find her. Since last night. Jules went to the police."

"I don't understand," Josephine said. "Where would she go?"

"We think she's been kidnapped," Martha said grimly. She glanced at Bran. "I must talk to you privately," she said to Josephine.

"He can hear anything you have to say," Josephine told her.

"But this is about—" Martha paused, then added, "Diego."

Bran and Josephine looked at each other and then at Martha. A wild supposition filled her mind.

"Bran is—" Josephine began.

Martha interrupted. "He's Diego!" she exclaimed. "But, then...." She frowned and shook her head.

"Then what?" he asked.

"Why didn't you—you could have come openly to Black Tor to see Josephine! All this secrecy...." She paused and took a deep breath. "Bill Wong's been shot—

did Josephine tell you? Now Sarah's gone. I sent Henry to the police with his suspicions of the man who passed letters to Josephine through Bill and Sarah. Diego. You, Bran.''

"Me?" His voice was incredulous. "Take that little girl? Shoot a man?"

"Diego—Bran—had nothing to do with that!" Josephine cried. "It's ridiculous!"

Martha watched him. Why had he waited all these years to come back to claim Josephine, and why had he done so in such a secretive manner?

"Why Diego?" she asked. "Why not come as Bran Lowrey? If that's who you really are."

Josephine's eyes flashed. "He doesn't have to explain anything," she said. "You don't know Diego or you wouldn't accuse him of—of...."

Bran turned to Josephine and touched her face. "Hey," he said. "Don't get so worked up. Martha's on our side— at least I think she is. She's worried about you. And about Sarah." He faced Martha. "I wouldn't hurt a child. Ever. I haven't even seen her since the day we all—wait!" He frowned. "In the tower," he said. "It couldn't have been you, Jo, because you and Martha must have been in the bedrooms by then. Your light was on there, I was watching."

"Diego and I were going to meet outside after supper," Josephine put in. "We had planned to before—before daddy and Simon and all. I thought the note on the whale was to cancel the meeting or something like that, and I...."

"I was waiting outside," Bran said. "I hadn't seen Jo since she sneaked back out after our trip to Craigdarroch Castle and we had to give you that fake story about her wanting me to take her into Victoria." Bran smiled. "We've had a problem with deception and wanting to see each other alone."

Josephine took his hand.

"I knew I was early last night," Bran went on, "but...." He turned to Josephine

Martha watched them looking into each other's eyes and felt like an intruder. Bran couldn't be acting. Or could he?

"I watched the light go on in Jo's bedroom," Bran said, "and I knew she was getting ready for dinner. Then a light went on in the tower. I saw a face pressed against the window. I was startled, thinking maybe you were there despite the light in your bedroom. But then the face went away and the tower light went off. Now that I know about Sarah, I think maybe it was her face I saw. Because she's dark like you, Jo. I got a quick impression of white face, dark hair."

"Had Sarah been in the tower with you earlier?" Martha asked Josephine

"No. I didn't see her after she came to my bedroom to tell me about Simon. If she really was in the tower, if that's who Bran saw," Josephine said, "I wonder why she went up there without looking for me in my bedroom first?"

"Maybe she wasn't looking for you," Bran suggested.

"But Sarah didn't like being up in the tower alone," Josephine said.

"Then Sarah must still have been in the house when the accident happened," Martha said, "because that was only a few minutes later. Josephine and I couldn't have been in our bedrooms more than ten to fifteen minutes."

"Another rigged accident," Bran said. "Someone wants Jo out of the way—permanently. Like before."

"You mean the drug overdoses?" Martha asked.

"Those, too, but I meant when she was taken away from Victoria and hidden in the U.S. somewhere—the time she can't remember. I came here from Seattle six years ago, trying to find her. She was gone, and I couldn't find out who she was. Did she tell you I didn't even know her last name? She thought I was dead, and I damn near was—in the hospital six months. So I gave up looking for her and went back to California, to San Diego."

"Bran put himself through the university working on the tuna boats," Josephine said.

"But I never was able to forget Jo and those—three days." Bran put his arm around Josephine. "Like a dream you always remember. Last year I came to Victoria on a vacation, and it wasn't long before I heard about Josephine Garrard, the princess in the tower. Someone pointed out Jules to me on the street, and I was almost sure. But then I had to leave—I had a job I needed. It took me another year to wangle this appointment to the museum, but this time I won't ever let her go."

A gray-haired nurse came into the room. "Oh, another visitor? I don't think Dr. Hansen...." She paused and assayed Martha, her eyes flicking over the sling.

"Martha's my nurse at home," Josephine said. "She was hurt, too."

"I see that," the nurse said.

"We appreciate you giving us a few minutes alone, Mrs. Freyler," Bran said.

"And those few minutes are all I can give you," Mrs. Freyler said. "I bent the rules a bit for that. But a fiancé...." She smiled at Bran, then looked at Martha. "I've been instructed by Dr. Hansen to keep all visitors out of Miss Garrard's room. But I called him about Mr. Lowrey, and he said that was all right. Even then, I should have stayed in the room...."

Martha nodded. "I'll just run along. Is there anything you need, Josephine?"

"No—thank you. They—they'll find Sarah, won't they?" Josephine's eyes were wide and frightened. "I couldn't bear to have her—hurt."

"The police usually find lost children," Martha said,

trying not to think of all the newspaper stories of molested mutilated children.

On her way out Martha stopped at the desk to inquire about Clara Eccles and was told that she'd been transferred to a nearby convalescent facility. Henry wasn't back with the car when she went outside, so she decided to walk the few blocks and see if she could talk to Miss Eccles.

Josephine's former nurse was in a wheelchair in the library of the convalescent hospital. Her face was lined and wrinkled, but her hazel eyes gazed at Martha with wary intelligence. Her manner warmed slightly as Martha talked about Josephine and her concern for the girl. Then, when she heard of last night's accident, Clara Eccles was obviously distressed.

"Oh, then it's still going on! I was afraid that would happen. Another accident." She gestured at Martha's arm. "And you, too. Like me."

Martha studied Miss Eccles, then made up her mind. "Do you think the cord was meant for you—that you were the one meant to fall and be injured?"

There was a silence.

"Louella's talked to you, I see," Clara Eccles said at last. "If Louella trusts you, then I shall. She's not likely to be wrong. Yes, I needed to be gotten out of the way. He would have preferred my death, but at least he succeeded in having me removed from Black Tor, which left Josephine unprotected."

"But another nurse would just be hired—as I was," Martha said.

"Yes, but a new nurse wouldn't be suspicious. He knew I was. I'd been asking questions—"

"*Who* knew?" Martha asked, interrupting.

"Why, Jules Garrard, of course."

CHAPTER TWENTY-TWO

MARTHA RODE BACK to Black Tor with her mind roiling like the water at the base of the cliff behind the house.

Jules. Could he be behind all the so-called accidents that had occurred in the past few years? Even his wife's fatal fall down the steps might have been planned, as Clara Eccles's had been. But why would he want his wife dead?

"I've been asking here and there," Clara Eccles had said. "People tell me things, once they learn I was injured at the Garrard house. There was gossip that Cynthia Garrard had lovers, that she and Jules weren't sharing a bedroom, that the baby Cynthia carried wasn't her husband's."

Martha thought of his arrogant face, the unsmiling dark eyes. Did he resent his wife's infidelities to the point of murder? And Josephine—was his greed for money so great that he wanted his half sister dead?

Jules had held her, kissed her. Martha's face burned at the memory. Had he made the gesture of love to bind her to him, keep her unsuspecting?

"There was talk that Jules's cousin was the father of Cynthia's baby," Clara had said.

Charn? Why did Jules then let Charn go on staying at Black Tor? Wait—Charn described himself as an errand boy. Was this deliberate on Jules's part—a continual humiliation of his cousin by reminding him that he, Jules, controlled the money and Charn was therefore dependent on him for everything?

Clara Eccles was certain that Jules wanted Josephine dead. "He'll make sure you leave," Clara had said. "Then some fatal 'accident' will happen to Josephine—wait and see."

In vain, Martha had mentioned Bran Lowrey.

"No one can protect her from Jules. He's too clever. The Garrards are ruthless, like the killer whales they resemble." Clara Eccles's face had crumpled and tears had come to her eyes. "But who will believe me? Even you don't."

Was this the reason Norman Garrard had been so afraid for Josephine, and why he hadn't confided in Jules? For fear that Jules was responsible for all that had befallen Josephine? Everything seemed to fit.

But then why had Jules run another ad for a nurse? Why had Jules hired her?

An insidious thought wormed into her consciousness: *you were hired because he knew you were Marty Collier. He investigated when he received the application you sent, and he found out. He wanted a nurse with a secret—with a dubious background.* If she'd had suspicions and had talked to anyone in authority, who'd believe Marty Collier?

Martha felt a sudden chill. Cynthia dead. Simon dead. Norman—but surely Norman's death had resulted from his illness. Hadn't it? Jules had been in the room. But she hadn't watched what he was doing. . . .

Martha stared unseeingly from the car window at the passing scenery, her eyes fixed on the horror within her mind.

Where was Sarah? How could the girl have been a threat to Jules? She saw again the eager face, the flashing grin that was Sarah's. Who would harm a child?

What could she do? Whom could she talk to? Dr. Hansen? He'd banned visitors from Josephine's room. Why?

She wasn't seriously hurt. Was the doctor afraid of an attempt on Josephine's life while she was in the hospital?

I can trust Dr. Hansen, Martha decided. *But will there be any use in telling him what Clara Eccles believes?*

Martha clenched her hands in her lap. *I'm afraid,* she thought. *Afraid Clara is right, afraid of what will happen....*

"I'm going to the woods again when we get back," Henry said suddenly. His voice startled her.

"To the woods?"

"Maybe Sarah's hurt in there somewhere. She always did like those woods. Not afraid of anything, she isn't."

"But the woods were searched last night and today, too, Henry," Martha said.

"I'm going to look, anyway," he said stubbornly. "When I called the hospital to ask about Bill Wong this morning, I wanted to know if I could see him, but they said I couldn't. He might know something...."

"I inquired about him at the hospital," Martha said. "He's still on the critical list."

She didn't see any way of telling Henry that the man he suspected of shooting Bill Wong and kidnapping Sarah wasn't guilty. She didn't believe that Bran Lowrey had had any part in either crime. Or in Josephine's "accidents." Diego/Bran might at the worst be a fortune hunter. Martha wasn't sure she quite believed his story of why he'd waited so many years to find Josephine, but he certainly would want her alive and well.

He'd been outside the house the night before, though, and he claimed he'd seen someone in the tower who could have been Sarah. Why would he lie? Martha sighed and decided to believe Bran. She'd go up to the tower and see if there was any sign of the girl. The tower had been checked, but she'd look again.

Once back at the house, Martha lost no time in climbing

to the tower and examining the room. She opened the window seats to check in the storage spaces—although Cathleen had said she'd done that the previous night—but they contained nothing but old books.

Was there anything to show that Sarah had been in the tower? Josephine's book still lay on the floor. Martha turned it up to see the title. *Growing Pains*, by Emily Carr. Oh, yes. The Victoria artist whose paintings she'd seen. Josephine had identified with Emily, with her struggles for acceptance. Strange, almost pagan landscapes—greens, blacks.... The paintings had been impressive.

The book dropped from Martha's hands. Nothing else there. A deck of cards, the stuffed parrot in its bamboo cage.

Wait. Josephine hadn't brought the cards. These were Sarah's. The last time Martha had seen them was in Sarah's room, strewn across her bed. Now they were there, in the tower. Had they been here earlier? *I'd have noticed them,* Martha told herself.

Then Sarah had been here in the tower while Martha and Josephine were changing for dinner. But where had she gone after that? Had she come downstairs in time to witness the whale falling and been so frightened she'd run off?

Martha shook her head. Not Sarah. She'd have been right there. She'd have scrambled down the stairs to be first on the scene.

Martha turned toward the steps. No point in staying in the tower any longer. Then she froze in position, listening. Was someone coming up? She took a step backward, holding her breath.

Who?

Had someone watched her climb to the tower? Martha tried to swallow, but her throat was too dry. But Jules hadn't come back to the house yet—it couldn't be Jules.

After a moment she gained enough courage to peer into the stair opening. She saw no one. She hurried down as fast as she could with her bandaged arm.

Martha locked herself in her bedroom and found that she was still clutching Sarah's deck of cards. She placed them beside her on the bed. Before he'd left that morning, Jules had said that Josephine was taken care of. What had he meant?

Josephine was certainly safe in the hospital with Dr. Hansen watching over her. Jules would be paying Mrs. Freyler, of course—Josephine had no money yet. So Jules could get into the hospital room. Did Dr. Hansen's order include Jules at all? Where was Jules at the moment; what was he doing?

There was a knock at her door.

"Who is it?"

"Cathleen. May I come in?"

Martha's impulse was to tell her no, but she rose and opened the door.

Cathleen entered, cool and watchful, dressed in the palest of blue pantsuits. Martha's eyes widened and Cathleen smiled.

"What did you expect—black?" she asked Martha. "I'm not Natalie, thank God. Norman is dead and nothing we do changes that. Why should I drape myself in mourning? I'm not that much of a hypocrite." She stood facing Martha. "How's Josephine?" she asked.

"She's—doing quite well," Martha said.

"Why did Jules leave orders that we weren't to visit her at St. Joe's?"

"Well, actually I think it was Dr. Hansen," Martha said.

"The hell it was. I heard Jules tell him on the phone to keep her room off limits to all visitors. How did you get to see her?"

"I was asked to leave by her nurse," Martha said. "But I did have a chance to see that she was all right."

"Do you know what's going on?" Cathleen asked.

"I—don't understand."

Cathleen waved an impatient hand. "The whale tipping over, Bill getting shot, Sarah gone. Why?"

"The money," Martha said. She didn't like Cathleen, but, oddly enough, she felt a need to talk to her. "Someone doesn't want Josephine to have the Garrard money."

Cathleen nodded. "But why Sarah? What's the connection?"

"I wonder if she saw something she shouldn't have," Martha said.

An emotion shone for a moment in Cathleen's eyes—fear? She turned away. "Well—thanks," she said, and moved toward the door.

"Wait," Martha told her. "Where's Jules?"

"I don't know." Cathleen's words were sharp. "He hasn't come back."

"Jules would have the entire Garrard fortune if—if anything happened to Josephine, wouldn't he?" Martha asked.

"Yes, I think so," Cathleen said, her voice so low that Martha scarcely heard her. Then she raised her head and surveyed Martha in her old imperious manner. "What's the matter—getting cold feet?"

Martha couldn't answer. Cathleen smiled crookedly and left the room.

Left alone, Martha became aware of a growing hunger. She'd missed lunch and hadn't thought to eat while in town. She unlocked her door and went downstairs to the kitchen, where she awkwardly fixed herself a sandwich with her one useful hand and poured herself a glass of milk. Carrying these on a small tray, she started across the foyer toward the stairs.

The foyer seemed larger than ever, empty and intimidating. All traces of the whale were gone. The house was quiet—a house of death.

The voice from behind her made Martha turn so fast she almost fell, and the milk slopped over onto the tray. Louella stood in the foyer. Martha had no idea where she'd come from.

"I—I was hungry," Martha said.

Louella paid no attention. "Jules should not break with tradition," Louella went on. "His father ought to be on the catafalque just there where the stairs curve. Abel lay in state there, as did Josie, Margaret and Cynthia. Norman should be there, too. I don't know what Jules is thinking, but then I never have. He was secretive even as a boy."

Louella moved closer to Martha. "Have they found Sarah yet?" she asked.

"I don't believe so," Martha said. "There's been no news."

"Natalie has poor judgment," Louella told her. "She was too severe with Josephine as a child, and now with Sarah—not enough discipline. Extremes. Always extremes. She was furious because Abel left her share of the money in trust with Norman in control. But her father knew Natalie only too well. No judgment at all. I blame her for Sarah's disappearance. Leaving the child alone at a time like that, after the shock she's suffered!"

"Natalie isn't at fault," Martha said. "She seems to be fond of Sarah in her way."

Louella gave an unladylike snort. "The only person Natalie has ever been fond of is herself. Of course, she's besotted over Matthew Drew—always has been since she first laid eyes on him, old as she was at the time. Anything Matthew does is wonderful."

Louella smiled. "He expected more than that trust fund of hers. I'm certain he did. Still, he's stayed on with

Natalie and taken care of her. But I've heard him fuss at Jules about needing more money. As if Jules could do anything with Norman holding the purse strings. The Garrards are generous only to a point. I never forget that. Look at poor Sarah.''

"What do you think happened to Sarah yesterday?'' Martha asked.

"Why, she ran off in a fright and now she can't get back here. She's lost somewhere.''

"Wouldn't someone have found her by now?''

"You'd think so, unless she's been hurt and can't tell them who she is. Or like Josephine when she was younger. Maybe Sarah has amnesia.''

CHAPTER TWENTY-THREE

MARTHA ATE THE SANDWICH in her bedroom, then lay on top of her bed, trying to rest. Images flooded her mind. Sarah's worried face peering into hers at the edge of the cliff on the day of the picnic, Bran's guileless grin as he introduced himself to her on the ferry from Seattle. Guileless! Josephine standing in this bedroom when they'd first met, Martha's coral necklace in her hand. And Jules. His face flashed before her—smiling, harsh with anger, cold, withdrawn, warm with affection. . . .

Martha sat up. She wanted no part of any of the family. If Jules were here, she'd tell him he had no need of her services any longer, and then she'd leave. Go back to Seattle, to safety with Ginetha.

When he returned, that's just what she'd do. Josephine had her Diego now; whatever Bran Lowrey's motives might be, he'd look after Josephine. And Sarah. . .Martha sighed. Her eyes went to the deck of cards beside her on the bed.

Someone knocked.

"Yes?" she called.

"I must speak with you immediately." Natalie's voice.

Martha opened her door. Natalie stood on the threshold with Matthew behind her.

"Now, Natalie. . ." he was saying.

"I expect you to pack and be gone by tomorrow," Natalie told her. "There's no reason for you to remain at Black Tor."

Martha stiffened. "I'll leave when Jules returns," she said. "He's my employer."

Natalie's face grew mottled with rage. The resemblance to Norman was very strong. "You'll do as I say!" she exclaimed, her voice harsh.

"Now, Natalie," Matthew repeated, "don't upset yourself. No doubt Miss Jamison has her own reasons for staying on."

"Slut!" Natalie cried, taking a step toward Martha. "You won't snare Jules with your wiles! He wants you gone, too—he told me so! Can't you understand no one wants you here? No thanks to you that Josephine isn't dead like her father. You're a poor excuse for a nurse." Natalie thrust her face near Martha's. "Get out!" she cried. "Get out or I'll have you put out!"

Martha fought down her anger. She looked at Matthew. "When will Jules be back?" she asked him.

He shrugged. "If you'll tell me where he went, I might have an idea when he'll return."

"I haven't seen him since early this morning," Martha said. "He didn't say he planned to be away overnight."

"The funeral is scheduled for tomorrow," Matthew said. "Certainly Jules will be here then." He took Natalie's arm and urged her away.

"Remember—you're to be out of this house by tomorrow," Natalie said. The color had drained from her face, and Martha realized that Natalie was really an old woman.

Martha watched Natalie carefully, alerted by the difficult rapid respirations, the slight cyanosis of the lips. Was Natalie suffering from the same illness as her brother? Matthew had said his wife had a heart condition.

"You'd better have her rest," Martha told Matthew, her ire muted by the realization that Natalie wasn't well.

He nodded, leading Natalie along the corridor. Martha watched from her doorway. Natalie moved slowly, leaning on him for support. Did Matthew have his wife under a doctor's care? She should be.

I'll talk to Jules, Martha thought, then shook her head. No. There'd be no conversations with Jules. She'd pack and be ready to go as soon as he returned.

I could move out of the house, anyway, Martha told herself. *There's no reason I can't rent a room in Victoria. I don't have to stay at Black Tor and wait for Jules.* But when she looked out her window at the long shadows falling across the lawn, her resolution faltered. *Tomorrow,* she decided. *I'll pack tonight and ask Henry to drive me to town in the morning. Natalie will be satisfied—I don't want to make the woman ill—and I can stay in Victoria until I'm able to give Jules my resignation.*

Martha sat on her bed and Sarah's cards scattered onto the floor. She knelt to retrieve the fallen cards, but as she tried to gather them, one jammed into a tear on another. Martha pulled them apart and as she did so a piece of one came off and fluttered against her. She picked it off and looked at the torn half of the king of diamonds. The card must have been ripped nearly through to have come apart so easily. Yet the deck was quite new.

"I pretend they're people I know," she remembered Sarah saying. "All the face cards, the kings and queens and jacks. 'Knaves,' Aunt Louella calls the jacks. Like in 'the knave of hearts he stole some tarts....'"

Who was the king of diamonds?

"Jo is the queen of spades because she's so dark and pretty and sort of sad...." Sarah's words again.

Why didn't I ask her who the other face cards were? Martha asked herself. Why had Sarah torn the king of diamonds? Did she mutilate it in fright or in anger?

"Maybe you can be the queen of hearts," Sarah had said. "She smiles nice like you do."

But who was the king of diamonds?

Martha laid the torn card on the bedside stand. None of the men in the household had a beard or a mustache. The diamond king had both. Of course, Bran had a beard, but he was young. Wouldn't Sarah place him as a jack?

Martha shook her head. Speculation was futile—the card could even have been torn accidentally. She glanced at her watch. Should she appear for dinner?

At first she thought she wouldn't go down, but then she decided she couldn't bear the entire evening alone in her room with the door locked.

Everyone was seated when Martha came into the dining room. A place had been set for her, and she slipped into it without looking at Natalie. There was also an empty place at the head of the table. Jules wasn't back.

Grilled salmon was the main course. Martha tried to enjoy the meal, despite the chilling silence at the table. Charn caught her eye once and smiled, but no one else acknowledged her.

In the silence the phone sounded with astonishing clarity. After a few moments Francis appeared. "A woman asking for Miss Jamison," he said.

Ginetha, Martha thought. *I haven't written her and she's worried.* She rose and followed Francis to the phone off the foyer.

"Are you Martha?" the voice said. A strange voice, one she didn't recognize.

"Yes, I'm Martha Jamison."

"She asked me to call you. I can't keep her here. The police will come, I know they will. I heard on the TV about her being missing. You have to help."

Martha clutched the phone with sudden hope. "Sarah?" she demanded. "Do you know where Sarah is?"

"She's here. She came last night and Jimmy hid her in his closet. I didn't even know she was here until this morning. I thought she had permission. But then I heard the

TV...." The woman paused, then added, "I don't know how she found the place, a little girl like her—she was only here the one time. She said a nice lady gave her a ride—she told the lady she lived here, can you imagine? Anyway I can't let her stay. My father's in the hospital, he might die and I just don't know what to do. Sarah said to ask for you."

"You're Bill Wong's daughter?" Martha asked incredulously.

"Yes. And my husband isn't home and I'm so upset and—"

"Is Sarah there? Can I talk to her?"

"She and Jimmy are outside—something about kittens. I want you to come and get her. Jimmy's too young to—"

"Where do you live?"

"Out on West Saanich Road. Do you know the Butchart Gardens turnoff?"

"I think so—at least Henry, the chauffeur, would," Martha said.

"Oh, no, you can't bring anyone else. Promise me."

"But—"

"Look for the sign that says Tod Inlet and turn there. Smithson is the name on the mailbox. Please hurry. I think Sarah knows something that frightens her. But I can't keep her—what if the police find her here?"

"But I don't have a car. I need—"

"I can't talk any longer," Mrs. Smithson said. Then the line went dead.

Martha stood for a moment undecided. Finally she went into the kitchen. Henry sat at the pine table in the center of the kitchen. Ruth had just taken up a platter of food and she stood staring at Martha. Elsa, the cook, glanced at her, then away.

Martha hurried to Henry and bent to speak close to his ear. "I have to have a car," she said, hoping her voice didn't carry to the women. "It's about Sarah."

Henry eyed her for a moment without speaking. Then he rose and beckoned her to follow him. He led her out a back door that Martha had never used before, and as soon as it was shut behind them, he turned to her. "What's this about Sarah?" he asked.

"I need a car. The woman I talked to said I had to come alone."

Henry tapped his finger against his chin. She could barely see him in the gathering dusk. "I don't suppose Mr. Jules would mind, seeing as how it's you," Henry said at last. "Come along to the garage. Do you know how to drive an Austin?"

"I won't have any trouble," Martha said. "I know stick shifting."

"Nothing's going to be easy with one hand. . . ."

"I'll be fine," Martha said, relieved that she wouldn't be responsible for a big car like the Rolls.

"Where are you going?" Henry asked.

Martha hesitated. "Out by Butchart Gardens," she said at last. "Maybe you can tell me how to get on West Saanich Road."

"That's 17-A," he said. "There's a map in the car." He paused, then added, "You're sure you know what you're doing, miss?"

"I'll bring Sarah back with me," she promised.

"Let me drive you, miss. It would be easier. Driving one-handed like you'll have to do, and shifting and all," Henry said, shaking his head. "You'd better let me drive you, miss."

"No, Henry," Martha told him. "I have to go alone."

At last Henry nodded, then led her past Cathleen's red car and a tarp-backed Land Rover—Mr. Drew's, Henry said—and Martha got into the sea-green Austin.

"Green's an unlucky color." Why did Josephine's words echo in her ears?

Driving along the narrow private road toward the highway, Martha had little trouble shifting, despite her useless left arm, and she gained confidence as she drove. She followed the highway signs to 17-A, and once she was on West Saanich Road, she tried to find a landmark she recognized. But Jules had driven Sarah and her to Butchart Gardens in daylight, and the darkness made a difference.

Where was the scarlet bed of salvia? Had she passed it? There was no way to tell. Despite her concentration, she almost missed the Tod Inlet turnoff. Once she had made the turn, she drove as slowly as possible, afraid she wouldn't be able to see the mailbox, much less the name.

Her eyes burned and her neck ached with effort by the time she finally spotted the fluorescent letters. J.E. SMITHSON. Martha swung the car into the drive.

Her headlights illuminated a small gray-shingled house set among evergreens. As Martha shut off the engine, the door to the house opened and a figure came down the steps.

Martha rolled down her window. "Mrs. Smithson?" she called. "I'm Martha Jamison."

The woman ran toward the car, around in front of the headlights, and Martha had a fragmentary impression of dark hair and eyes. She reached the driver's side and clung to the door.

"I'm May Smithson," she said. "Thank God you came. Sarah and Jimmy aren't back. I'm so frightened."

"Where were they going?" Martha asked.

"To find a kitten Sarah said she'd seen. I thought she meant out in the field behind the house, but I called and they haven't come."

Martha looked into the black eyes so near hers and felt at a loss. "Is Sarah all right?" she asked.

"Yes, she's fine. Something had frightened her at home, someone with a crazy name, it started with Al—I don't remember."

"Ahlmakoh?" Martha asked.

"That's it. But where are they, where's my Jimmy?"

Something flickered in Martha's mind. Kitten. A kitten.

"How near are we to Butchart Gardens?" she asked.

"Less than a mile. But you don't think...?"

"When we visited the gardens the other day there was a kitten in the arbor by the refreshment stand. Sarah was quite taken with it."

"But that's a long way. And it's dark. Jimmy knows better—"

"Why don't you get in the car, May, and we'll drive over."

"Oh, no, I don't think I'd better. What if they come back and no one's here? Besides—the gardens? They wouldn't be there—it costs money. I don't see how you can be right...."

"I'll go over, anyway, and look."

"Oh, I wish Jim wasn't out on the boats," May said. "I'm scared."

May's fright spread over Martha like a fog. She started the engine, a sense of urgency making her heart beat faster. What if the children weren't at the gardens? Where would she look next? Had someone taken both the children?

Ahlmakoh? What did Sarah mean? Just that she was afraid of the unknown? But the rest of the myth crept into Martha's mind. Ahlmakoh, the woods demon who devoured lost children....

CHAPTER TWENTY-FOUR

THERE WERE SEVERAL of the double-decker tour buses along with a sprinkling of private cars parked in the lot outside Butchart Gardens. Martha remembered Jules saying the tourist season ended soon, and certainly there was no crowd that night. She parked and hurried toward the entrance. The arbor and the refreshment stand weren't far from there, as she recalled.

A young man in uniform stood at the stand, leaning on the counter and laughing with the woman inside.

"Have you seen a little girl—and a boy?" Martha asked. "They're six and eight. The girl has dark hair with a white streak in it."

"No, miss, I haven't," the man said.

"Wait—I think I might know who you mean," the woman said. She leaned across the counter. "I saw two kids playing with one of the stray kittens that hang around for handouts. Seems to me they went up toward the house. I thought it was odd they were alone."

"Did the girl have dark hair with a white streak?" Martha asked.

The woman shrugged. "I didn't notice that close. If you take this path—" she pointed "—you'll come to the house."

Martha thanked her and hurried along the footpath with boxwood hedges on one side and hanging baskets of geraniums on the other. "Sarah?" she called, once, twice. There was no answer and she met no one.

She could see the thin outline of a cypress above the roof of the rambling house and remembered the tree was part of the Italian Garden. The Rose Garden would be to her left. Would Sarah have gone to either of those?

Martha shook her head. Impossible to tell where Sarah might be. Was she wasting her time there? Surely May Smithson had been telling the truth—or had she?

Suddenly uneasy, Martha glanced behind her along the walk. Still, she reassured herself, May hadn't mentioned Butchart Gardens at all—that had been her own idea.

Sarah had said something about a favorite place there—hadn't it been the Japanese Garden? Martha remembered the girl jumping from one stone to another across the creek. Where was the Japanese section? Past the Italian Garden somewhere.

As Martha started down a path that seemed to lead toward the cypress, lights glared in her eyes. She recalled Jules telling her that the lights were arranged for maximum effect if one went through the gardens following a designated path. She must be heading backward, against the lights.

"Sarah!" she called.

She skirted the lily pond, then hurried through the Italian Garden, past the Frog Fountain, and saw the Japanese Garden bridge from the top of a flight of steps.

Martha paused and looked down, shielding her eyes against the lights. Had she heard a child laugh?

"Sarah?"

Silence.

"Jimmy?"

"What?" The boy's voice came faintly.

Martha sucked in her breath and started down the stairs.

"It's Martha," she shouted. "Don't be afraid, Sarah."

When she reached the lacquered bridge, she turned her back to the lights and looked about her. After a moment, a small figure slipped from behind a clump of bamboo and approached.

"Martha?"

"Oh, Sarah, is it really you?"

The girl began to run, then flung herself at Martha, grasping her tightly. But then Sarah let go and raised her head as though listening. Quickly she glanced about her.

"Did *he* know you were coming?" Sarah asked.

"Who?" Martha asked, her heart sinking. Who else could Sarah mean except Jules?

Sarah didn't answer, continuing to look all around. "It's okay, Jimmy, you can come out," she said at last.

Jimmy came from between rhododendron bushes; he was a dark-haired boy not much larger than Sarah. "I heard someone coming," he said.

Sarah clutched at Martha's hand, tugging at her, urging her toward the clump of bamboo.

"That's a good place to hide," she said.

"But who are you afraid of?" Martha asked.

"Him," Sarah said, her eyes on the stairs.

Martha followed her gaze and saw a figure outlined against the lights at the top.

"He saw us," Jimmy hissed. "We gotta run for it."

Sarah dropped Martha's hand and darted away to follow Jimmy, who was already running. They headed deeper into the gardens, and as Martha hurried after them, she tried to recall where the path led. Through the Rose Garden? Then where?

She looked behind her and saw that the figure was halfway down the stairs. A man? Some of Sarah's urgency filled her, and she increased her pace, running, calling to the children to wait.

She passed hedges, flower beds, trees, all with the lights glaring at her, traveling backward along the night-tour route, heading—where?

A sign loomed to her right: THIS WAY TO THE SUNKEN GARDEN. And that was at the base of the old quarry. Somewhere soon she should come to Ross Fountain— "magnificent at night," Jules had said. Was he behind her this very moment?

Martha caught up to Sarah and took her hand.

"What are you afraid of?" she asked, but the girl didn't answer, just hurried on. Jimmy ran ahead.

They passed a group of people headed in the opposite direction. Martha could hear the muted roar of the fountain before they rounded the last turn and saw the colored lights. Another group led by a uniformed tour driver was just leaving the rail where they had gazed down at columns of water reaching seventy feet into the air, changing sequence as the multicolored lights played against the spray.

"Come on," Sarah said. "We can't stop. He—"

"Well, you two, you've led me a merry chase!" Not Jules's voice.

Martha turned still holding on to Sarah, and saw Matthew Drew. Jimmy was nowhere in sight.

"I worried about your driving alone with that broken collarbone," Matthew said as he came up to them. "Why didn't you ask me to help? And Sarah—scaring us all for no very good reason, I'll wager."

Martha glanced at Sarah, who was staring at the ground. The girl didn't answer but slumped against Martha as if exhausted.

"I—didn't have time to ask for help," Martha said, trying to see Matthew's expression clearly. "How did you know where I was?"

"Henry told me you'd taken the Austin to Butchart Gardens," he said, "and I saw the car in the parking lot when I got here. Why on earth is Sarah here? How did you know...?"

"There was a phone call," Martha said slowly. "Sarah

was visiting Jimmy Smithson—you know, Bill Wong's grandson.''

Matthew squatted and tried to peer into Sarah's face, but she buried it against Martha's side. Martha felt the child tremble.

''You frightened us all,'' Matthew said to Sarah. ''Why did you run off?''

Sarah didn't answer.

''She's exhausted,'' Martha said. ''And no wonder, with all the—''

''I'll carry her,'' Matthew said, and scooped Sarah up into his arms before Martha could agree or disagree.

She tried to see Sarah's reaction but could not.

''There's someone else with us,'' Martha said to Matthew.

''Who?'' His voice was sharp.

''Jimmy Smithson. He was with Sarah.''

''Why don't you find him?'' Matthew said. ''I'll take this tired little girl back to Black Tor while you drop Jimmy off at his house.''

Sarah raised her head from Matthew's shoulder and Martha saw that the child's eyes were wide and staring, her face rigid with fear.

Of Matthew?

Martha hesitated, unsure. Why would Sarah fear Matthew, her Uncle Matthew who told her all the Indian legends about Ahlmakoh and Shishchuikul, the demons of the woods and mountains?

''I saw you,'' Sarah said to Matthew, her voice high and thin. ''You put that paper on the whale. And you looked up and saw me on the stairs and you said a bad word and you scared me like that time in the woods when Josephine fell off the cliff, and then you told me it was Ahlmakoh, only it wasn't—it was you—so I hid in the attic and I tore your card up because I didn't like you anymore. After I came down I heard the noise and I saw Jo and Martha and the whale all broken, and you tried to catch me and so I ran away.''

"Let her go! Let her go!'' Jimmy erupted from the darkness and flung himself against Matthew, kicking and hitting.

Instantly Sarah began to struggle in Matthew's grasp and squirmed free, only to fall sprawling on the cement. She cried out once, then lay still.

Crouched over Sarah, Martha stared up at Matthew. "Get some help!'' she demanded.

"Not likely,'' he said. He bent over and picked up Sarah's limp form.

Martha rose to her feet, stunned by what had happened, by the realization of what Sarah had seen him do.

Matthew was responsible for the whale falling on Josephine. And for the other "accidents''? Had he shot Bill Wong? Killed Simon?

"Let me have Sarah,'' she said, her voice choked.

Matthew laughed.

Jimmy! she thought. Without turning her head, she shouted, "Run, Jimmy, run for help!'' She took a step toward Matthew.

Matthew moved to the railing and leaned over, holding Sarah poised above the empty space. "Cooperate and I won't drop her,'' he said. "And no use yelling for the boy—I fixed him.'' He jerked his head to the left, and Martha saw Jimmy's body beside the path. Was he dead?

If only someone would come....

"Don't—please don't!'' Martha begged. "She's only a little girl.''

"Ah, but whose little girl?'' Matthew said. He shifted Sarah in his arms.

"Oh, no, please—I'll do anything you say,'' Martha told him.

He looked at her. "If you agree to come with me back to the car and not scream or attract attention, I'll bring Sarah with us."

"What—what will you do then?" Martha asked.

He smiled, but it was really more of a grimace. "You'll have to take your chances, won't you?" As he spoke, he moved back from the rail and she saw him slip something in his pocket. Did he have a gun? Bill Wong had been shot....

"I—I'll come quietly if you don't hurt Sarah," she said.

The journey was a nightmare through the beauties of the Sunken Garden...the exotic trees and plants like growths from another planet, the lights blinding her, her mind numb with fright. They passed no one; it was getting too late for people to start the tour.

Martha glanced at Matthew from time to time. Had that been a gun in his pocket?

"You're wondering about me," he said as they hurried past beds of blue ageratum and blazing salvia. "You're asking yourself why." He laughed. "Why do you think?"

Martha swallowed and finally was able to speak past the dryness in her throat. "Money," she said.

"Of course."

"But—Simon?" she asked.

"Simon reported to me—for money. Then he found out about Sarah. An accident—the old man didn't mean to let Simon know. After that I couldn't afford to have Simon around. I couldn't trust him not to tell someone else who Sarah was. So I poisoned him. Quite easily. He popped pills, as the saying goes. I emptied his capsules and refilled them."

Matthew's pace began to slow. There was a hedge along the left-hand side, and Martha tried to recall if that meant they were almost to the parking lot. He kept her ahead of him, so she had no chance to try to get his gun, if indeed he had one.

"You don't ask what I learned about Sarah," Matthew said. "I shall tell you just the same. She's Josephine's illegitimate daughter."

"Josephine! But—"

"Of course, Josephine doesn't realize—she has no memory of that time in her life," Matthew went on. "But when I discovered this, I knew Sarah must be gotten rid of, as well as her mother. Too bad—I like children."

Martha shuddered. Jimmy's crumpled body back by the fountain, and Sarah so nearly over the edge there. How could Matthew say he liked children?

Matthew's steps slowed still more, and Martha knew he was tiring. The unconscious Sarah was a heavy weight.

Martha walked a little closer to him. "I thought Jules got all the money if anything happened to Josephine," she said.

"No." Matthew spoke with some effort. "Natalie. Money reverts to Natalie. Norman's idea of playing fair."

"Did you shoot Bill Wong?" Martha asked.

"The bastard tried to blackmail me. Saw me on cliff with you. Remembered Josephine almost going over. Saw me then, like Sarah did. Asked for money the other day." Matthew stopped walking.

I could run, Martha thought. *There must be people in the parking lot. Would he shoot? And what would he do with Sarah if I did get away?*

"You carry Sarah," Matthew said. "We're almost to the car." He draped the girl over Martha's shoulder and she sagged under the deadweight. Then he pulled the gun from his pocket.

"We'll use the Land Rover," he said. "I wouldn't try to yell for help. I'll see the two of you dead before they get me." He stepped behind Martha again.

As they came around the final curve in the path, a woman came toward them.

"Remember," Matthew said softly.

"I see you found the little girl," the woman said, and Martha recognized her as the one from the refreshment stand.

"Yes," she said.

"How about the boy?" the woman persisted.

"Oh, He—he's gone," Martha said.

Then they were in the lot. The tour buses had left, and the Austin and Land Rover sat side by side. Matthew led her toward his vehicle.

Someone opened the door of the Austin as they approached. Matthew froze.

"I've been waiting for you," May Smithson said to Martha. "I just couldn't stay—"

Martha wrenched herself away from Matthew and agonizing pain tore into her shoulder as she thrust Sarah at May.

"Run!" Martha screamed. "He's trying to kill her. Run!" Then she turned and threw her whole weight against Matthew.

He struggled with her, trying to push her aside, but Martha clung to him as long as she could, until at last he flung her against the side of the Land Rover. She couldn't catch herself and fell heavily to the asphalt. Shouting and screaming filled her head as the blackness closed in. Her last thought was the fear that May hadn't managed to get Sarah away.

CHAPTER TWENTY-FIVE

MARTHA WAS BACK in the nightmare with Johann. Disembodied voices, great colors bursting in her head—had Johann managed to sneak a hallucinogen into her food again? She was swaying, drifting away from the earth. Words broke like soap bubbles and spattered her with droplets of meaning:

"...hospital...."

"...serious...head...bloody shame...."

Blood. No longer bright and fluid with life, the red changing, becoming rust, sticky to the touch... Johann floating in his own dead blood, and she was too late, forever too late....

"...gun...."

No, not a gun. Johann had used a knife—the Thai dagger he affected as a letter opener, its bronze handle etched with a many-armed god who had no power to save him, either. "The kindest use a knife because the dead so soon grow cold...." Wilde had said that in a poem. What had he meant—that dying by degrees, death in life, was worse? He was wrong, wrong. The dead stay alive forever in the mind; they never grow cold....

"...remember...."

Josephine doesn't remember. The years are lost. Josephine. Martha struggled to recapture her thought. *Josephine doesn't belong with Johann. He's gone, the years are gone. This is another time....*

"Martha." Not Johann's voice, and yet a man she knew.

"Martha. Can you hear me?" Jules's voice.

Martha opened her eyes. Jules's dark eyes were inches from her own. She was lying—where? On the ground. Why was she on the ground?

"I know you're in pain," Jules said. "But try to think. Do you know where Jimmy Smithson is?"

The night's events raced back into her mind. Sarah and Jimmy—the fountain—Matthew....

Where was Sarah? Martha tried to rise, but the pain in her arm and shoulder stopped her. Her head throbbed.

"Don't move," Jules warned. "We're waiting for an ambulance. Can you remember about Jimmy?"

"I—he—near the fountain," she said, her head pounding with the effort to force out words. "Matthew—by the fountain."

"Jimmy's near Ross Fountain?"

"Yes."

Jules turned his head and spoke to someone else. Martha heard the words but they had no meaning.

"Jules," she said. "Don't go away...." Martha wanted to reach out and touch him, but her eyes closed and she drifted away again. She wanted to hold on to Jules but could not. Jules was not for her, not for Marty Collier....

When Martha came to awareness again, she was in bed. The walls around her were green and she was gazing at a picture of Mary holding the infant Jesus.

Hospital? she thought. *St. Joseph's?* She raised her head a few inches from the pillow to look around. Yes, a hospital room. Sunshine was outside the window, a piece of blue sky. The night before was over.

"Martha—you're awake!" Josephine's voice was warm,

and as Martha turned around, Josephine leaned over and kissed her.

"You're all right," Martha said. "You're dressed." She felt stupid, her mind still foggy.

Bran stood alongside Josephine. "Thank God you're all right, too," he said.

"There won't be a scar," Josephine told her. "Dr. Hansen said so himself."

A scar?

"Does your head ache? You're frowning so." Josephine leaned over her again. "Do you want the nurse?"

Martha started to shake her head, then realized something was wrong. Her left hand was bound across her chest but she could move her right arm, and she raised her hand to her head, encountering cloth—a bandage? "Did I hurt my head?" she asked.

"A cut across the temple—I think they shaved off some hair," Josephine said. "Dr. Hansen said you had a concussion, too."

Last night, Martha thought. She'd been lying on the ground and Jules was there. And.... She struggled up onto her right elbow. "Where's Sarah?" she demanded. "Is she...?"

"She's here in the hospital," Josephine said. "I—we've just seen her. They've moved her out of intensive care and she's conscious. She told me she was hungry."

"And Jimmy?"

"His mother took him home this morning. Just a bad bump on the head, I guess. He was—hit with something."

The gun, Martha thought. Jimmy was hit with the gun. She had to try twice before she got the next name out. "Matthew?"

"He's dead," Bran said. "Ran into the woods and shot himself."

There was a moment of silence. "Do you—know about Matthew?" Martha asked at last.

"Jules told me—told us." Josephine took Bran's arm.

"About—Sarah, too?"

"Oh, she'll be fine," Josephine said. "She does have a skull fracture, but it's only a hairline crack across the side of her head. Dr. Hansen says not to worry."

Martha stared at Josephine. Obviously she didn't know about Sarah being her daughter. Did Jules? Did anyone else? Her eyes shifted to Bran and he grinned at her, and Martha suddenly realized what was familiar about Sarah's wide smile—her mouth was like her father's. The resemblance shone clearly when they smiled.

"Daddy's being buried today," Josephine said. "So many terrible things have happened. I hope that his funeral is the last of death."

Matthew needs to be buried, too, Martha thought, but she said nothing.

"I'll come back and visit you as soon as I can," Josephine said. Her face clouded. "I still don't understand about Uncle Matthew. Not really."

"The money," Martha said.

"Yes, I know that. Jules explained. Poor Jules—I've blamed him all along." Josephine shook her head. "But why would Matthew need more money than Natalie has? Why would he try to—to kill me to get it?"

"Jules told us Matthew wanted more money for his Indian research," Bran said. "He'd turned down Matthew's requests for more money just as his father had always done." Bran shrugged. "After all, Matthew had no credentials in the field—he was an amateur."

Why, you intellectual snob! Martha thought, for a moment forgetting her terror of Matthew the night before.

"Matthew was a fanatic," Bran went on. "Any research he did was biased, slanted the way he wanted to see it. A hobby—that's how he should have viewed what he did. Instead...."

A fanatic. Yes. Martha closed her eyes, remembering the terrible moment when she'd thought he would drop Sarah off the edge above the fountain.

"You're tired," Josephine said. "We have to go, anyway."

When they were gone, Martha rang for the nurse and asked her to try to get a message to Jules Garrard. "Tell him it's about Sarah," she said.

Josephine and Bran had to be told they were Sarah's parents as soon as possible. But she wasn't the one to tell them. She had no doubt that Matthew's information through Simon had been correct. Everything fit. She'd let Jules know, and then he'd have the responsibility.

The day passed, and Martha dozed and ate and dozed again. Dr. Hansen came in to see her and let her walk to the bathroom, and she found that the trip left her only a trifle dizzy. Josephine didn't return as she'd promised, and Jules didn't come.

Day edged into night.

Does Jules think I'm going to be an embarrassment? Martha wondered. *Hanging on him, begging him not to leave me as I did last night?* Her face flushed as she recalled her plea.

He needn't worry about having her return to Black Tor. As soon as Dr. Hansen would release her, she'd head for Seattle and convalesce in Ginetha's apartment. And then....

And then what? Martha took a deep breath. She shut her eyes and Jules's face was there in her mind. Would it always be?

When she awakened, she thought at first she was still dreaming. Jules's dark eyes looked into hers; his fingers stroked her cheek.

"Oh!"

"I didn't mean to startle you," he said, and sat back in the chair he'd drawn up to the bed.

"I—I asked you to come because of Sarah," Martha began. "Matthew told me that Josephine—"

"I came because I wanted to see you," Jules said. "I couldn't get away earlier."

"But you don't understand. Josephine is Sarah's mother. She...."

Jules sighed. "I've just finished talking to them—Josephine and Bran. They're completely overwhelmed. Josephine was all for rushing back here and having an emotional reunion with Sarah, but of course we convinced her that she couldn't. The poor child—what will she make of it?"

"Sarah loves Josephine."

Jules nodded. "But Josephine as a—a mother?" He turned his hands upward.

"She has Bran now," Martha said. "And she'll grow up once everyone quits protecting her as though she were still a child herself."

"Did Matthew tell you how he found out?" Jules asked.

"From Simon. Somehow Simon extracted the information from your father. That, and about the will—about Natalie getting the money if Josephine died." Martha frowned. "I can't understand why. If your father knew about Sarah, why wouldn't he have her inherit?"

"I'm not sure," Jules said. "I suspect he thought an illegitimate child should have no rights—he was very old-fashioned. And then, too, he didn't know who Sarah's father was. Josephine thought her lover was dead, so there was simply no other information."

"How did you discover all this?" Martha asked.

"In my father's safety-deposit box. I was able to have it opened yesterday. He left a detailed letter in the box for me, telling me how he located Josephine soon after she ran away from Black Tor,'' Jules said. ''He found her in Seattle, and when he had a doctor see her, he discovered right away that she was pregnant. Josephine was incoherent much of the time, but she did say her 'Diego' was dead.

''When Sarah was born, he placed her in a home there in Seattle, intending to bring Josephine back to Black Tor. Josephine by now was living in another world, scarcely aware of what went on around her. Father certainly had no idea she would run off again. Even then he'd probably have found her, except she got in with one of those commune families who were going back to the land in Oregon. It took him over a year to trace her. Luckily she'd been treated fairly well.''

''And Josephine still remembers none of this?''

Jules shook her head. ''I'm going to have Louis—Dr. Marston—see her again with all the facts available. Perhaps he'll be able to help her retrieve the missing memories.''

''Your father never did acknowledge Sarah, then,'' Martha said. ''Why did he bring her to Black Tor?''

''After he eventually found Josephine again and brought her back, he went back to Seattle and took Sarah to a new foster home in Victoria. He wrote that he finally brought Sarah to Black Tor when he saw it would be obvious to everyone that she was a Garrard. She developed the white streak in her hair when she was about two.''

''It seems so unnecessary,'' Martha said. ''All the secrecy. Bran acted equally clandestinely, sneaking notes to Josephine and sighing them 'Diego.' Why didn't he simply come for her?''

''He was years finding who she was.'' Jules shook his head. ''What a romantic pair, the two of them—and so foolish, wasting all that time.''

''But once he did know,'' Martha said, ''why not march up to Black Tor and ring the doorbell?''

"Bran says he heard stories in Victoria about Josephine being shut in the tower—can you imagine—and having a keeper so she couldn't ever leave the house. He thought he might not be let in to see her, and of course I suppose he wondered if she really was mentally ill. He didn't admit to that. He's all right, though—had a rough time getting where he is in life. A hard worker."

"He'll be good for Josephine," Martha said. "You do see that."

Jules sighed. "I'm glad she's off my hands. I've never known what to make of her since father brought her back home—sarcastic one moment, a whining child the next and then, seemingly without effort, a poised young woman."

"How is—Natalie?" Martha said after a few moments.

"Broken up, of course," Jules said. "But I also have a feeling she's curiously relieved. As though she'd known something was wrong but hadn't dared ask what. There's no question that she loved Matthew. While he treated her well enough, I don't believe he really cared for anything but his Indian research."

The way I love you, Martha thought, *while you care for—what?* "I'll be leaving sometime next week," she said. "Dr. Hansen wasn't sure of the exact day, but—"

"Nonsense. If you need a nurse, we can have one at the house. Will can certainly see you there if need be."

"But, Jules, there's no need for that—I'll soon be well enough to fly to Seattle and—"

Jules leaned across the bed and took her right hand, holding it between both of his. "You belong at Black Tor," he said. "I want you to be my wife."

Martha stared at him, speechless.

"Well?"

"I—I won't have all those stuffed animals around," she said at last, unable to speak the words of love that almost choked her.

Jules began to laugh. "I've swept out the remains of the killer whale," he said. "You may dispose of the rest." Then his smile faded and he looked into her eyes, and she saw the warmth and love in his face. "The time of hiding and pretense is over, Martha. Come to Black Tor with me and we'll begin again with no clinging to what's past."

I've been preserving my own past, Martha told herself. *Keeping Johann's memory around like the Garrards kept their stuffed pets. Not letting him go, letting him rest.* Jules was now; Jules was waiting for her; love was waiting.

"Yes," she said. "Oh, yes, Jules."

Harlequin Photo Calendar

Turn Your Favorite Photo into a Calendar.

JULY 1984

The Browns

Uniquely yours, this 10 x 17½" calendar features your favorite photograph, with any name you wish in attractive lettering at the bottom. A delightfully personal and practical idea!

Send us your favorite color print, black-and-white print, negative, or slide, any size (we'll return it), along with **3** proofs of purchase (coupon below) from a June or July release of Harlequin Romance, Harlequin Presents, Harlequin Superromance, Harlequin American Romance or Harlequin Temptation, plus $5.75 (includes shipping and handling).